# UTAH JENNINGS

# The Invasion

# 1

# Chapter 1 Descent into the Underworld

The Lineage Connection

*Alex is related to this woman. (4 months)*

Alex has been trying to share this stuff with these other people. Alex has been trying to visit these different websites. I'm not sure if this website is called Android.org. These people can try to trace anyone's else lineage to these other golden days of Jesus Christ. Alex might have some sort of connection with these other members of this lost tribe. Alex was trying to mention this stuff to these other people. They were trying to discuss these other topics amongst themselves. Someone else has told this gentleman. Judith might have been able to conceal this treasure chest on some long-forgotten island. If Alex can't verify this information through this company. Judith could have been another descendant of this gentleman's relatives again, fellas. Joseph was speculating about it again fellas. How Alex has related to this young lady's ancestor again, folks. Joseph doesn't know for sure if he could use this information to benefit himself. Joseph is waiting to try to sell this hidden treasure to another artifact dealer. I'm not sure if these other people are finding this stuff alluring to themselves. Joseph has learned about there is this holy Grail. Judith has been trying to hide these other objects underneath the earth's surface. Joseph was becoming another very wealthy person. Alex was disregarding these other people's feelings about his friend's plans for the future. These other people were threatening to take this person's life. Joseph wasn't interested in being sincere with these other people. Alex doesn't want another person to acknowledge his friend's past transgression over the years. Alex has been expressing his disapproval of his friend's actions against these other innocent victims. Alex was trying to explain this stuff to these other people. Alex was surprised that this situation was becoming a dire issue for these two people. Joseph is feeling a little drowsy this evening again, folks. Someone else has been demanding this person take another short nap this evening. Joseph was drifting along into this different world. Joseph has been fixated on this stuff ever since yesterday. Joseph has found out the location of this mysterious place through many of his other multiple sources. Joseph was encouraging these other people not to become so very naive around these other people's families again, fellas. Joseph believed that many of these other natives had these large bones protruding out of both sides of their cheekbones again, folks. Joseph wasn't interested in getting familiar with any of these other people's cultures again, folks. Joseph doesn't know anything about them and these other people's customs again folks.

## Dreams in the Dark

*Joseph wanted his cellmate to try to interpret many of his dreams for him. (9 months)*

Alex was telling another inmate about himself. Whenever someone else has woken up this guy from another nap again folks. Alex was taken aback by these two people kissing each other lips in this public setting again fellas. Chelsea was showing her lover some of her affection again, folks. Chelsea was going to be trying to remove her underwear for her boyfriend. "I'm not going get thrown into this same situation with you," Joseph said. Chelsea was very cautious of this other person. "I'm not approaching anyone else's daughter again, buddy. Hillary is another current member of the House of Congress" Alex said. Alex was responding to his friend's question about another person's transgression against these other people. "Hillary might have been influencing these other politicians' decisions for them. These other politicians have given this woman authority over them. Clifford is the former president of the United States of America. Chelsea must have caught her parents red-handed again, buddy. Hill might have been visiting this island. Jeffrey Berated is the owner of the island. This jury was able to convict this guy of these other numerous criminal offenses against his unsuspecting victims," Joseph said. "However, if you haven't read about this person's indictment on some of these different criminal changes again, buddy. Hillary could have been partaking in these other criminals' offenses with her husband's friend. These policemen weren't interested in providing this stuff to any of this person's other victims. This judge is sending this guy to a jailhouse," Alex said. "Jeffrey isn't above the law again buddy. I'm not identifying these other aliens for anyone else. I don't possess the same level of these other people's naivety again, buddy. We needed to keep this other stuff in our minds again buddy. Joseph, these other people wouldn't have considered this stuff to be fantastic for themselves. If this attorney wouldn't charge these two fugitives with these other criminal offenses against their victims. This judge shouldn't have proceeded to go through with these other people's court trials. If we're living amongst these other people. Whenever they are accusing these other celebrities of committing another criminal offense against their friends. These other senators should have removed most of these other politicians from servicing their other political opponents" Joseph said. "You aren't going to be able to offend me. If they're going to be having these other irrational thoughts about this woman's daughter again fellas. I'm not sure if Joseph this stuff is unlike me. If you weren't being discredit with your other sexual escapades with these other women. These other people are very perverted human beings. Hillary might have been exhibiting her other immoral behaviors towards her husband friends. I'm not destroying these other people's reputation amongst their friends. I'm not going to try to characterize them. These other people have their own sense of their immortality again, buddy," Alex said. "They're facing these other numerous repercussions from many of these other judges. I'm on another quest of mine. So, I'm finding the location of this person's holy Grail. I should have been able to obtain this person holy Grail for myself. I'm trying to ensure my own immortality again, buddy," Joseph said. Alex isn't accepting the fact that many of these other people are working against him. Joseph is intrigued with his friend's passion toward his missionary work again fellas. Joseph is eagerly trying to decipher the meaning behind this person's existence again fellas. Joseph has been sharing another small portion of his dream with his friends.

*They are very arrogant people. (9 months)*

Chelsea is this very conceited person. Chelsea has demonstrated this love for this craft to her both of her parents. Chelsea had these other ruthless intentions toward these other people. They were being exposed to many of these other characters. Chelsea was watching this stuff play out across this theater screen. Chelsea was making these other disparaging remarks about these sorts of characters. Chelsea wasn't satisfied with the plot of this movie. Wasn't Chelsea interested in trying to watch the ending of the movie? This director was trying to generate some sort of extra revenue for himself. "If they aren't willing to try to hire these other decent writers. If this screenwriter was trying to create another more effective way of capturing each of these other members' attention with this very low-budget film. "Who is this rodent?" Chelsea said. Chelsea isn't concerned with this gentleman's unartistic endeavor again fellas. "This rodent isn't this realistic killer. This rodent isn't satisfied with his life. he doesn't know how he going to be able to turn his life around in time" Chelsea said. This rodent wasn't able to try to persuade any of these other members of the audience. " I'm not sure if this rodent has any sort of parental guidance in his life" Chelsea said. Chelsea wasn't able to define this plot of the movie to anyone else again, fellas. "This rodent doesn't like to be hanging around these other worthless characters again sweetheart. If these other characters are trying to mess with this rodent plate of cheese again sweetheart. This rodent will be trying to butcher them. This rodent isn't going through these other ordeals by himself. This rodent was born with this speech impairment again fellas. "This owner is changing everyone else these other very outrageous prices to watch this movie. Because everyone else is feeling excited about seeing the ending of this movie. This director has made this very low-budget film. We're being surrounded by some of these other very low-class types of people. I'm not remaining amongst them," Brandon said. Brandon is inquiring about how his girlfriend's father's presidential campaign is doing right now these days. Brandon has these two very large chips placed upon both of his shoulder blades nowadays. They're very snobby types of these people. I'm not mingling with many of these other moviegoers. Alex has been able to ignore them. Alex wasn't enjoying watching this movie. Chelsea was trying to spoil these other moviegoers' experiences again, fellas. Alex wasn't willing to try to sit there quietly with them. Chelsea was seizing onto her boyfriend's two very large testicles again fellas. Chelsea was trying to massage both of her boyfriend's very large testicles again fellas. Chelsea was extracting her boyfriend's protruding penis from this pair of wrangler jeans. Alex was trying to avoid them. Alex was standing up for himself. This usher shouldn't have let these two people use the restroom. These two people were interested in indulging themselves. Chelsea was trying to perform these other sexual acts upon her boyfriend. Alex was staring a hole through them. Brandon was showing his very large penis to every single person again fellas. Chelsea was waiting to try to emasculate her self-proclaimed boyfriend. Brandon was able to try to push his girlfriend's large head forward against the center of his crouch again fellas. If Chelsea wasn't interested in trying to prevent another disaster from happening to themselves. They weren't disappointed in themselves. They weren't feeling disgusted with themselves. Chelsea didn't need to pause for another second again fellas. Chelsea was able to try to jump into the center of her boyfriend's lap. Chelsea was trying to ride him. This employee wasn't able to try to approach these two people. These employees weren't trying to eject those two people from this movie theater. This user wants another employee to try to bleach down these two people's seats again, fellas. I'm putting this other shit nicely to you.

## *Alex was sitting amongst these other three movies goer again folks. (9 months)*

Alex was walking around in the theater. Alex is earning his degree in computer programming again folks. Alex was being observant of these other movie posters. They were displaying these movie posters upon the movie theater wall. They were showcasing these actors and these other variety genres of film. They are anticipating a very large crowd. They are giving these other moviegoers their own cinematic experience again folks. They were buying their movie tickets from an employee of the theater. Alex was expecting to watch every exciting scene from this particular movie. Before Alex was entering this small room. Alex bought this can of soda pop again folks. Alex was getting himself. Folks a large bucket of popcorn. Alex was sitting amongst them. Alex is hearing this woman's voice vibrating throughout the hallway. Alex was smelling some woman's perfume floating from across the theater aisles. Chelsea was heading toward him. Chelsea wasn't softening the mood again folks. Chelsea was causing a distraction again folks. This movie theater was like this echo chamber. Chelsea was giggling at her boyfriend. They weren't capable of conducting themselves in any professional manner. They were making these other very loud noises again folks. Alex wasn't able to endure these other people shanagon again folks. Alex wasn't amused with them.

## The Theater Incident

*Joseph was imagining becoming a member of Hillary's family again folks. (9 months)*

Hillary has given birth to an daughter again folks? Joseph is wanting to implant his own seed inside of this woman's uterus again folks. Joseph is wanting to have a very large family. Joseph is desiring to pursue an romantic liaison with this person's daughter. Joseph has been thinking about them. Joseph is needing to change his behavior toward them. Joseph is giving up on this concept of being someone's father again folks. Is Chelsea capable of forming another romantic connection with another human being again folks? What if Chelsea is thinking about castrating him? What if Joseph's wasn't capable of getting an erection himself. Joseph was sweating profusely again folks. Joseph would have preferred to taste this woman's uterus again folks. Joseph is wanting someone else to marry him. "You haven't been reading any of these other newspaper articles yet buddy," Alex said. Chelsea is getting engaged to another college student. I'm thinking this college is located somewhere in the state of Ohio. Hillary is on the campaign trail" Alex said. Alex must have shown his other friend a photograph of this young lady. "If I'm in your position again buddy. I wouldn't have gone anywhere near this snobby little bitch" Alex said. "Why you're commenting on this snobby lady's appearance again buddy," Alex said. " I wouldn't have been in this lady's life," Joseph said. Joseph is getting into a big mess with them. "I'm not letting these other people to fuck this lady again buddy. If they're giving you and my other friends a rabies shot again buddy. Because you're needing to get it again buddy" Alex said. "Chelsea isn't going to be attractive to me. Chelsea has this gross looking face in my opinion again buddy" Joseph said. " I'm not saying anything else about them. I'm not going to be assassinating this lady's character again buddy. I'm staring into Satan eyes again buddy? " I'm not overreacting about it myself. I'm warning you. I'm wanting you. Alex to proceed with caution again buddy. before you're entering into this very dark hole. You're being surrounded by these other devilish looking people again buddy" Alex said. "So, you're going to be telling me. You're not letting your friend photos end up on any missing persons flyer. If you're not able to lay your own eyes upon them. I'm remembering the good times that we're sharing between the both of us. We could have been drinking a few cans of these beers my friend. Whenever you're reflecting upon my memories again buddy" Joseph said. " I'm thinking about you. I'm taking myself. Joseph a very short nap again buddy. you shouldn't have been letting anyone else to disturb me. I'm appreciative of you" Alex said. "You shouldn't have allowed anyone else to approach them. Whenever I'm being released from this prison. I'm finding this shit very interesting to me. What If they're not wanting to accept anyone else as a part of their own family again buddy? I'm not returning to this lady's house on Christmas Eve. I could have been doing this shit to them. I'm thinking about removing this lady's underwear from her waist again buddy. I'm not an employee of this woman's family foundation" Joseph said. Joseph heard his friend. Joseph snoring away again tonight folks.

*Joseph was talking about this lady daughter with his own friend. (9 months)*

They're sitting on their cots. They were talking about these politicians amongst themselves. Alex has met with them. Joseph is wanting to wrap both of his hands around this lady's throat again folks. Joseph might have enjoyed choking this lady to death again folks. "I'm not doing these other horrible things to them. We're in serious trouble with them" Alex said. Nobody else knows this lady whereabouts again folks. Someone else has told these people so much about them. Someone was going to be calling them. They are traveling to this other region of the world. Joseph has gone with him. Alex haven't seen them and these people friends at their relative Jewish bar mitzvah. "You haven't mentioned this other stuff to me" Joseph remarked. "You're not a member of the Jewish community" Joseph said. "I'm not a Jewish person. I have seen this lady's daughter at the movie theater. Chelsea was watching some sort of scary movie with her boyfriend. Chelsea has invited her own boyfriend. Brandon to sit beside of her at the movie theater again folks. They were holding the other person's hand again folks. Chelsea was kissing him. They don't know Where they are going to be at any particular moment of the day again folks. They could have said something else to him. They didn't excuse themselves. "I'm not watching this shit taking place in front of me" Alex said. Alex is harboring other jealous feeling towards them. "You're becoming frustrated with them" Joseph said. " No, I'm not feeling comfortable around them. They are embarrassing me" Alex said. Brandon was discreetly placing both of his hands underneath his girlfriend dress again folks. They were forcing these other people to observe them. Alex wasn't able to obtain any photograph of this young lady's uterus again folks. Alex wasn't sending his friend any other copies of this young lady's photograph again folks. "You are looking very disgusting to me. I'm not going to be enjoying myself. If I'm watching you, or someone else fucking some other young lady in the pussy again buddy. I didn't notice it was them" Alex said. Joseph was licking a large portion of his own finger again folks. Joseph was making these other offensive hand gestures towards him. Joseph was wanting to fuck them. "Chelsea's pussy is looking very hairy to me. What if Chelsea's isn't shaving a small portion of her own pubic hair again buddy. Chelsea isn't waxing a very huge portion of her own pussy hair again buddy" Joseph said. Joseph has been willing to offer these two people his services again folks. "Chelsea might have been wanting to get someone else to trim her pubic hair for her again buddy. Besides if you're insinuating this other stuff to me. I might have known about the length this woman's pubic hair again buddy. you're sadly mistaken about it again buddy. I'm developing my own sets of principles again buddy. so I'm gonna want to get everyone else to follow these principles of mine" Alex said.

*Joseph is thinking about escaping from prison. (1 year)*

"These two fugitives are accompanying my partner to our van. I'm going to be able to handcuff these two suspects" this policeman said. I'm trying to restrain these two suspects. These two fugitives are getting anxious about these other things again buddy. I'm trying to separate both of those suspects. I'm not sticking both of these two fugitives together into the same jail cell. Alex doesn't find these two police officers' ideas appealing to him. This judge didn't grant these two fugitives any of their other repeal requests again, folks. So they weren't able to try to appeal this judge's decision against them. So, these two suspects aren't going to overturn this verdict against themselves. This lawyer was trying to help these two people by presenting their two cases to another judge. They weren't able to receive another fair trial again, folks. Alex doesn't need to be living beside a serial killer. What if this person had killed this other numerous amounts of other people during his lifetime? This person was able to try to target another person. This person shouldn't have been bothering them. Jeffrey was eating another large portion of his other victim's flesh again, folks. "You have gotten this overactive imagination again, buddy. You were overreacting to this situation again buddy. Jeffery doesn't like to try to eat on the flesh of another alien" Alex said. "I'm thinking of escaping this prison. I'm not enjoying myself. Joseph my friends shouldn't have been confined with someone else. If they weren't trying to shoot me. I don't care again buddy. I'm not refinding this situation for anyone else. I'm not taking these other chances with anyone else. I'm breaking out of here soon, buddy. I'm not living another large percentage of my life with these other inmates. I'm not going to be able to take another prisoners hostage again buddy. But I'm not doing this other stuff alone again buddy" Joseph said. This person has been grabbing ahold of this guy's arms again folks. These two people have been forcing these two fugitive to accompany them. Alex prevented his friend from being injured by these two policemen. Because they were going to be forcing his friend to get down on the floor. Alex wasn't going to be able to stop them. They were going to be elevating this man's feet off the ground. They were trying to smash their pistol against his friend's forehead again, folks. "I'm not going to be allowing these two guys to do this shit to us," this policeman said. They were instructed to follow these two policemen's instructions again, folks. These two policemen were placing these two fugitives in the back of the vehicle. Whenever they arrived at the prison. These two policemen were telling these two fugitives to stay with them.


## *Hillary speech (1 year)*

Hillary speech (1 year)

Hillary was establishing her political career. Hillary was becoming another very influential person. Hillary was taking these other jobs seriously again, folks. Hillary is facing off against her other political adversaries. These voters were developing these other lower expectations of many of these other politicians. If Hillary wasn't trying to finish her other political commitments to these other politicians. Hillary has been exerting pressure upon them. Hillary is assisting her other employees again, fellas. I'm not sure if many of these other voters weren't expecting their favorite candidate to win this upcoming election. Hillary is going to be able to pursue her other political ambitions again folks. Hillary wasn't worried about the safety of these other people and their children. These two fugitives weren't able to affect these other people's opinion of this politician. Hillary has put in place her contingency plans for her future. I'm not sure, folks, If these other voters were supportive of this woman's political endeavors again, fellas. Hillary's campaign manager was working alongside this woman's other employees. If Hillary hadn't used these other methods to sway some of these other voters' opinions of her political status. Hillary isn't conveying these other messages to many of her supporters. Hillary and her campaign manager were developing this more effective plan for themselves. If Hillary isn't focusing any of her other energy on completing many of these other tasks of hers again, fellas. Hillary is going to be able to accomplish many more great things during her lifetime. If Hillary isn't getting many of these other people to vote for herself.

Hillary was investing most of her husband's other money into these other worthwhile charities. Hillary was traveling alongside each of her many other employees across this entire country. Hillary was going to be expressing her other political beliefs to many of these other supporters of her again fellas. If they weren't advocating on their favorite candidate's behalf. Hillary does have many of these other separate ideas from everyone else, again, folks. Hillary isn't the perfect candidate. Hillary isn't achieving most of her other dreams again, fellas. So they are going to be able to develop an outreach program for many of their supporter's children. Hillary is improving these other people's lives. Hillary was offering many of these other people another incentive to work in these different meaningful jobs. So if they don't work a little harder than everyone else on this planet. They won't be able to have access to the dream again fellas. These other people weren't interested in trying to thrive within our tough economy again fellas. Hillary wouldn't have been able to reward many of her other employees for trying to excel within this political landscape again fellas. Because these people were trying to contribute anything else of them to this person's political campaign. I'm not sure if these voters aren't interested in electing this woman to any sort of administration. I'm not sure if these other people are interested in attending these other candidate's political rallies. This person wasn't trying to raise some funds for his other favorite politicians. If Hillary isn't interested in trying to strengthen the sovereignty of this nation. If Hillary can't fix many of these other people's problems for them. If Hillary isn't interested in addressing many of their other concerns for them. I'm not sure if these other people are going to be hindering their children's ability to reach their fullest potential in this world. Hillary has been able to generate these other new opportunities for most of her other supporters. Hillary is trying to alleviate some of these other people's financial burdens again folks. If Hillary isn't trying to balance the budget for these other citizens of this country. Hillary hasn't been making any sort of effort to try to rebuild this country's ecosystem again, fellas. Hillary depends upon these other politicians to help her friends to try to stabilize our citizen's future. If Hillary isn't using her other common sense again folks. Hillary isn't interested in trying to stop the decline of these other people's morality. If Hillary isn't willing to try to address this situation amongst themselves. Hillary isn't sure if these other people are eroding the fabric of our society. Hillary was experiencing these other devastating consequences within her lifetime. "I'm not another person's mentor. I'm not helping these other politicians to become victorious in their other political endeavors again, fellas", Hillary said. Hillary was trying to unleash these other natural catastrophes upon these other communities. These voters don't need to try to listen to this woman's other political rhetoric again, folks. If Hillary isn't producing enough jobs for these average citizens. Hillary isn't the person. Hillary was the sole proprietor of a major corporation. Hillary isn't allowing someone else's father to be clinging to her two massive bosoms. Hillary was bolstering to many of these other people again folks. These other women should have been trying to provide nourishment to many of their other children. These other people aren't changing some of this woman's other political agendas. These people weren't looking at some gentleman's girlfriend's breasts anymore, folks. Hillary is interested in making these other people defenseless against them. These gentlemen's wives aren't complaining about their husband's behavior toward their children again, folks. These gentlemen aren't interested in mistreating many of their children. They aren't capable of improving their own lives. If Hillary isn't interested in harming these other people's reputations within this political landscape? If these gentlemen are not fighting this person for their companion's other freedom. If these other gentlemen are going to be able to reiterate against their wives again, folks. Because these other gentlemen aren't the oppressors of these other women. "Because I've got an objective in my mind again sweetheart. If I'm not trying to defend our taxpayer's root principles anymore again, folks. I'm developing other diverse programs for you. I'm planning this mission of mine. I'm continuing to support them. If they're not shaving their hairy pussy again folks. They aren't capable of doing this shit alone again folks. These other people aren't capable of influencing anyone else again folks. As they were watching the crowd of people. They aren't spotting them. If they aren't exposing their wife's bosom to them. Nobody else shouldn't have an issue with me" Hillary said. Hillary is glancing into this person's camcorder.

Hillary isn't spreading this other nonsense amongst them.  Hillary isn't a very good liar.  " If I'm not creating another strong foreign policy.  If I'm not capable of persuading them.  I'm not becoming a very decent person.  Clifford is preventing these other men to fuck me.  I'm making an example of these other people again folks.  I'm wearing the pants in my family?  Clifford doesn't exhibit any self-control again folks.  If I'm not going to be ascending to heaven.  I'm going to be singling out them.  I wouldn't have voted for them.  You aren't obligated to me.  They shouldn't have allowed these women to fulfill their mission on this planet.  You shouldn't have allowed these women to be offensive to you.  I'm not insulting your guy's companions.  If they aren't capable of being appreciative of you.  Because they aren't turning over their body to another male.  Clifford is expecting these other women to participate in these childish games with them.  Clifford has been enjoying watching his secretary's breasts bounce up and down again, folks.  They aren't letting these other men play with their wife's breasts anymore again folks.  They need them.  They're ruining the stock market again folks.  I'm not letting these foreign rulers have a sexual encounter with me.  Do you wish to learn more about yourselves?  I'm not keeping doing this crap to myself?  I'm not subsidizing this other foreign terrorist.  They could've been fighting alongside us.  So we're restoring these other individuals' sovereignty ourselves.  If they're not sharing their property with their wives.  They don't need the resources to fight them.  They might've won the war again, folks.  They're continuing to gain momentum against us.  We have given these people the legal right to carry their firearms.  If they're choosing to impersonate these magical ELFs themselves.  They shouldn't have been allowed to get drunk with them.  If they're putting a baby diaper on their counterpart again, folks.  They're manufacturing these products again folks.  They're making these diapers to fit around a baby butt again, folks?  If they're choosing to undertake their children's minds again, folks.  If they're choosing to let another guy smack their wife's asses nowadays, folks.  Nobody should've intruded on their wife's lives again, folks.  I'm making prognoses with this millennium again folks.  If I'm obliged to obey them.  I'm bringing these policies of ours to fruition again, folks.  I'm changing the country's direction again, folks.  I'm not getting rid of these people again folks. If they don't agree with my ideology again, folks? We can't afford to allow these other people to move forward again folks. I'm not restructuring these methods of mine. I'm demanding these foreign leaders place restrictions on their citizens. They don't need to have access.


## Forbidden Desires

*Joseph is insulting the family members of these two guys himself (1 year)*

A policeman is accompanying these two gentlemen. They are locking these two fugitives up in a jail cell. The policeman wants someone else to facilitate this process for them. Whenever this judge is willing to try to execute most of her other duties again folks. This judge needs to try to fill out these other necessary documents herself. The policeman is engaging in this other conversation with these two fugitives. They aren't seeking this other person's perspective on the matter again, folks. These two fugitives are waiting to try to communicate with most of their other relatives again folks. They aren't capable of arranging this shit themselves. These two fugitives weren't allowing this policeman to try to expedite them. They were becoming a little impatient with these two policemen. These two fugitives can't try to explore these different options for themselves. Alex isn't sure how complicated this situation is getting between themselves. Alex believes this stuff is another foregone conclusion, in his opinion again, folks. The policeman is requesting to try to speak with his supervisor. The policeman must have tried to explain this stuff to his supervisor. The policeman is trying to send these other messages to his supervisor's email address again, folks. The policeman isn't updating his other files. someone else needs to get into contact this wife. This woman doesn't want to fuck these two fugitives. This policeman isn't going to be treat those gentlemen unfairly again folks. This woman hasn't gone through similar experiences with these two fugitives. Joseph has been waiting to try to stick his penis insides of this woman's uterus for a while again folks. This policeman must had a very small penis again, folks. Joseph was trying to describe this policeman's sister to his friend. These two women breasts are the same size of two of these large melons. Joseph has been waiting to suck upon this woman's breasts again folks. While this woman is trying to fondle this creature. Does Alex want someone else to watch these two people fucking each other again fellas? "Maybe you're getting another chance to try to taste this lady's pussy for yourself," Joseph said. "you shouldn't worryingly about me," Alex said. Alex refuses to allow three of those other inmates to sleep with them. They aren't capable of fucking three of those other inmates. Whenever they are going to be entering into this prison system? They were referring to two of those other inmates. As fresh meat. "You're going to become another inmate's little bitch," this policeman said. "I'm partaking in another orgy with them. I'm going to be thinking about it again buddy. I'm going to be inviting many of those other females to come over to my house. I'm fucking this young lady's brain out of her head again buddy. I'm imagining this woman's breasts bouncing up and down against my face. I'm allowing this lady to suck my very large penis again buddy? I'm cummin in this lady's mouth again, buddy," Joseph said. They weren't pleased with them. Because they were making these other offensive jokes at their sister's expense again, folks. " You shouldn't provoke them. They could've ripped off your heads by using their bare hands again buddy. If you're not stopping it again, buddy," Alex said.

*Joseph was praying to his friend's savior. (1 year)*

This person has been watching these two fugitives. But who is this person? They weren't going to be dying in prison. Joseph wasn't expecting his friend to be getting any of those other noteworthy results again, folks. Was Alex having these other issues with these other people again fellas? Alex wasn't gazing at his reflection in this mirror. Joseph wasn't interested in sharing many of his other secrets with these other people. Joseph is this alien. Alex was learning these different things about his friend's lifestyle. Joseph's brain cells might not have been functioning properly on him. Alex wasn't doing anything terrible to these other people's families. Alex was able to study these different types of species' mating habits with some of their other counterparts. This scientist wasn't able to try to transfer this alien's brain into another human being's skull. Alex might have been a little more intelligent than some of these other species. Joseph wasn't able to participate in many of those other scientists' experiments with his friends. This scientist was able to create some sort of truth serum again fellas. These scientists weren't testing any of these other drugs on their other patients. This scientist wasn't injecting these two fugitives with any sort of large needles again, fellas. Joseph shouldn't have been lying to them. These policemen weren't interested in someone else refuting these other gentlemen's claims about themselves. Joseph wasn't interested in addressing his other issues with this other person. Joseph has been able to create this dilemma amongst everyone else. These two fugitives have been able to share these coherences between themselves. Folks if this policeman wasn't able to discover this hidden information about these two fugitives. If this policeman wasn't interested in catching these two fugitives in the act of committing any of their other criminal offenses again fellas. If this judge wasn't interested in convicting these other fugitives. If they were trying to make these other false accusations against their other victims. If this policeman had tried to prove this stuff to these other jury members again fellas. If this policeman doesn't have any sort of evidence against these two fugitives. Joseph hasn't been traveling to these other planets. Because Joseph is trying to destroy this planet. Alex was considering if he should take many of those other college classes during the upcoming fall semester. Joseph wasn't being very supportive of his other friend's future endeavors again fellas. Joseph wasn't able to make another person his number-one priority over the summer. These other professors weren't interested in being helpful to their other students. Because many of these other students have been developing their other life-changing ideas again, folks. Alex recognized there was this clear distinction between his anatomy and those other species's anatomy. Alex was lacking this attention span again folks. Alex wasn't able to try to process some of this other information within his brain again, folks. Alex doesn't try to comprehend many of those other college subjects again folks. These other professors weren't able to reach through their other student's minds. Alex wasn't enjoying this wonderful weekend again fellas. I'm not sure if many of these other professors were interested in trying to developed these other students curriculums again, folks. I'm not sure if many of these other college students were interested in trying to learn about these other species mating habits again fellas. Alex was swaying back and forth in this chair. "If you're feeling anxious about something else again buddy. Because If you weren't able to grasp many of these other concepts about these other people's lives in general again, buddy. I'm receiving this very good education," Joseph said. "I'm feeling slightly puzzled about this other stuff again buddy. I'm not sure if many of these other professors were interested in teaching their students these other specific college courses throughout any sort of specific region. You weren't having this natural reaction to them. Whenever I'm going through these similar experiences as you. I'm going to be able to pray for your sister's health again fella" Joseph said. Joseph wasn't trying to fold both of his hands together. "Amen, I'm putting my faith in my friend's savior," Joseph said. These two fugitives weren't walking into these similar areas together. These two fugitives were having an conversation amongst themselves. Alex should have been able to process this amazing power within himself. Alex wasn't speaking to anyone else about their situation again fellas. Nobody else was able to pay.attention to anyone else. "I'm not going to be apologizing to theses other people for my friend endangering their lives," Alex said. "I'm not letting another person to try to get anything else past me," This policeman said. Alex was staring at his dog's pictures again fellas. Alex was doing those other wonderful things to try to help these other people's families. Alex mother did accomplish these other amazing things during her lifetime. Alex was able to try to graduate from this particular university.

*The judge has sentenced these two guys to five years in a federal prison herself. (1 year)*

On September 30th, 2022, they underwent this fair trial. The jury has rendered another guilty verdict against them. Because this judge has found those fugitives guilty of committing this criminal offense against an employee. This judge has sentenced both of them. They were given the maximum penalty to understand the law of their state. This judge has granted these fugitives this opportunity to address the entire courtroom. Before the judge was able to try to discipline these two fugitives. They were allowed to assert their innocence to each member of the jury. "Hillary was trying to accuse me and my partner of committing many of those other criminal offenses against many of these other victims. I'm not going to be engaging in any other type of criminal activity with any of my other friends. This judge wasn't being decisive enough toward us" Alex said. This judge wants this policeman to drag those fugitives into her courtroom. "I'm not going there alone again fella. I'm going to be trying to express my dissatisfaction with the members of this jury again fella. I'm not going to let these other people carry out this miscarriage of justice against me. This judge shouldn't have been able to convict both of us. I'm screaming at these other people. I'm tired of going through this entire process with my friend. These other members of the jury. They might have formed their own opinions about the both of us. This judge wasn't an impartial participant" Joseph said. " If Hillary isn't interested in trying to file these other criminal charges against both of us. Joseph has been trying to coerce everyone else to work against me. I'm not allowing my friend to achieve many of his other objectives during this period again fellas. I shouldn't have trusted many of my other friends. This judge isn't acknowledging that I'm guilty of committing these other outrageous criminal offenses against these other politicians. I'm not receiving any preferential treatment from them. I'm trying to become fully committed to the improvement of my life" Alex said. "Alex, you don't have any sort of testicles again folks. Alex is a rotten excuse for another human being. I'm not an associate of my friend. I'm not going to be able to try to serve this long prison term for anyone else. I'm turning over a whole new leaf again folks," Joseph said. Alex was nodding his entire head the entire time again fellas. They don't believe these two fugitives' excuses again, folks. "If you aren't interested in trying to rehabilitate yourself," Alex said. "They shouldn't have been trying to force me and my partner to stay in these inhabitants. Because I'm leaving on another long vacation. I'm asking these other relatives of mine. If they would try to take care of my pet for me. While I'm gone away awhile again, buddy," Alex said. "I'm going to be dropping off your pet at this animal sanctuary," Joseph said. "I'm going to be facing these other injustices in the future. If these other people were trying to transport my partner dog to this animal sanctuary," Joseph said. "I'm not getting rid of my dog anytime soon again fellas. I'm going to be missing my dog. I'm calling upon these other people for their support during this difficult period of mine," Alex said. Trinity was licking this person on the palms of his hands again, fellas. Trinity wasn't allowed to play fetch the stick with her owner. "If this judge is sending me and my partner to this penitentiary. If we aren't able to get out of this messy situation with them. I'm not able to try to take my dog walking through this forest. I'm not going to become observant of many of these other religious holidays," Alex said.

2

# Chapter 2 Tension in the Cellblock

Confessions and Accusations

*I believe that there are these two policemen. (1 year)*

Are these two fugitives arriving at the courthouse? This policeman is trying to retrieve these two fugitives from the back of his van. Joseph was able to convince these other policemen not to be transporting him and his cellmate to the jailhouse. Whenever this policeman was unlocking these other fugitives' jail cells for them. These two fugitives were being detained with these other inmates in there again fellas. "I'm going to expect these two fugitives to turn around for me. So I'm trying to place these handcuffs around the wrists of these two fugitives. I'm trying to inform these two fugitives of their other constitutional rights to receive fair treatment from me and my fellow employees. If you aren't interested in doing something else terrible to these two fugitives. I'm not supposed to injure another person. Whenever these other prisoners are in my custody again fellas. I'm going to be expecting that you're going to try to cooperate with me" the policeman said. "I'm trying to ask these other policemen another question about how I have ended up in here again buddy. Before these other people are trying to sort out their differences

21

amongst themselves. Before I'm accompanying these other inmates into the courtroom. Someone else should have been serving these two meals to both of us. I'm getting very hungry this evening again, buddy," Alex said. "you have already eaten a bunch of this other food again buddy. You might have been able to gain some of this extra body weight again, buddy," Joseph said. "I'm getting tired of trying to fix these other inmates' problems for them. You are always complaining to these other inmates about your other roommates. I'm not willing to try to consume another large percentage of the food alone again buddy. This policeman shouldn't have placed another person in this room with me. I'm not on another strict diet again, buddy. I'm not allowing another person to try to limit my friend's food intake again, buddy. I'm trying to make some of these other decisions for my friend" Alex said. "You aren't walking ahead of me," this policeman said. The policeman told this stuff to these other two fugitives. They didn't make it out to this policeman's vehicle. If these two policemen weren't interested in doing these other underhanded things to both of these two suspects. This policeman wasn't trying to correct his behavior toward these two fugitives. So whenever this policeman started up his car engine.

### They appear in the courtroom themselves. (1 year)

September 10, 2022. They went through enough stuff again today. Because they can't attend football games again folks. Because they're not supposed to appear in a courtroom. if they weren't physically there again folks. A Policeman would've arrested them. They're escorting these two fugitives into the courtroom. Alex's steps were heavy with apprehension again folks. They're walking through a deserted hallway. They're having a different experience than everyone else again folks. As they're filing into the courtroom. They're dreading going through it again folks. They're guiding these two fugitives to their seats in the front row. this judge was towering over them. They're intimidated by this lady's presence there again folks. They're taking a deep breath again folks. So they can compose themselves. they're waiting for the proceedings to begin again folks. This police officer's presence served as a constant reminder to them. They're in some serious trouble with these police officers. They would've had to face the consequences of their actions again folks. They had this looming trial ahead of them. They believe that this stuff would've determined their fate again folks. As they sat there in silence again folks. Joseph's mind was racing with uncertainty and fear again folks. whatever happened in this courtroom. They believe that it would've had a profound impact on their lives again folks. This judge has exuded her authority over them. whenever she walks into the courtroom. whenever this judge demanded that these people focus their attention on her again folks. As this judge takes her seat on the bench again folks. This judge requests those other people in the courtroom to take a seat. These members have provided these people with these benches. Alex believes that these places were designated for these individuals. So they can observe the proceedings of the courtroom. The judge's request is not only a formality again folks. but everyone else is sitting comfortably in the courtroom. This judge is getting ready to hear these lawyers give their opening statements on behalf of their clients. They believe that everyone else is equal in the eyes of the law again folks. They must treat these two fugitives with respect under the law. The judge's simple gesture highlights her professionalism again folks. She knows the importance of maintaining order in the courtroom. This judge believed that it set the tone for a fair and just legal process for all these parties involved in this investigation again folks. " You must have a seat again buddy. Because the court is in session again fellows" the bailiff said. "I want the bailiff to tell me. which court cases are on the court docket first again buddy" this judge said. The clerk handed this judge a folder again folks. The clerk, a middle-aged man with a stern expression on his face again folks. This man has approached the bench. He has been working tirelessly to prepare for this moment again folks. This man carefully organized it and he has been reviewing these several documents in the folder. this man felt a sense of relief washing over him. They believed that this was a crucial piece of evidence in their case again folks. this lawyer made sure that every detail was accurate and in order again folks. The judge, a wise and experienced woman, accepted the folder with a nod of her head again. This judge is beginning to review the folder contents again folks. The lawyer's efforts would've contributed to the administration of justice. since the lawyer believed that this case's outcome depended on the judge's decision again folks. This lawyer knew that his part in this process was vital again folks. So he watched with bated breath again folks. The judge carefully reviewed the evidence against them. After she goes through the folder one last time. the judge gave the clerk a small smile again folks. The judge believed that this decision was hers to make against folks. but the court clerk had done his part again folks. This man made sure that this judge had access to the information she needed to continue this trial again folks. " I'm going to personally call out these people's names again folks. if they're present in this courtroom. Please if they could raise their hands in the air for me. If they can do this shit for me. Does this person exist again folks? Alex Jones is this guy's name again folks" this judge asked. "Is this guy here again today folks?" This judge said. Alex is lifting both of his hands in the air again folks. "If this person is present with us. I need to know this information for the record again folks. this guy's name is Joseph Flaggan" this judge said. "If this person could raise his hand in the air for me." Gentlemen and ladies, Joseph didn't want to raise his right hands again folks. Joseph wasn't obeying any of this judge's other orders again folks. "I'm asking these two fugitive to approach this bench," the judge declared. They ascended to the bench. "I'm asking these two fugitives a question again folks. If you're desiring to have a lawyer to legally represent you. Alex with this matter again buddy. If Alex your lawyer is entering a not guilty plea on your behalf" This judge stated. "They ought to respond to the judge's question on their own accord again folks." This lawyer said. "I'm not pleading guilty again today sweetheart," Joseph said. " I'm asking them. if they're going to be able to afford their legal representation again folks. I'm making an effort to appoint these two people an attorney again folks?" stated the judge. Alex remarked, "I don't have the budget to hire a lawyer again lady." Joseph stated, "I need this judge to assign me. Sweetheart an attorney." "I'm demanding that this bailiff take these two fugitives into custody again folks. They're remaining at the police department. I've set a new court date for a later time again folks.

I'm planning to schedule it for September 30, 2022. They're taking these two fugitives to this holding cell again folks. I need to speak with these two police officers" this judge said. "I wanted this policeman to take these two fugitives back to the jail." The bailiff remarked, "they're going to need to follow me." This bailiff said. This man led these two fugitives to detention again folks. " They should've been placed under mandatory lockdown again folks," this judge said.

## *Someone has brought these two guys their meals fellows. (1 year)*

Someone else has offended these two fugitives again, fellas. Alex wasn't present there again, folks. Alex was refusing to answer this policeman's question again folks. Alex wasn't trying to cooperate with these two policemen. This policeman proceeded to try to arrest these two fugitives. "I haven't been able to commit any other criminal offense with my friend," Alex said. Alex was questioning this policeman's integrity again, folks. Is this policeman opposing this gentleman? These two fugitives weren't able to get involved in this policeman's investigation again, folks. This policeman was using these other methods on these two fugitives. So if this policeman can't prove any of this other stuff to this judge again fellas. If this policeman weren't able to locate these other witnesses. So they can't get these witnesses to corroborate these two fugitives' whereabouts for them. If these two fugitives weren't doing anything else during this period in their lives. This policeman might have been able to inquire about these two fugitive's presences at this specific location. These two fugitives might have another friend. Who is connected with this terrorist organization? "If you don't know anything else about it again, buddy. Why do you want to try to steal any of these other documents for yourself? They were informing us. Someone else might have been letting your friend try to go through another person's file again, buddy. Because you didn't know who this computer belongs to again, buddy," This policeman said. This person might have been able to confirm it through someone else. If this policeman were getting his information through these other multiple sources again, buddy. This person is an employee of another agency. Joseph was awaiting his release date for quite some time again folks. "I'm not returning home," Joseph said. I'm not sure if folks this information is based on this policeman's observation of these two fugitives. This policeman hasn't been authorized to try to release any of these other inmates from the prison. These other inmates aren't interested in trying to be tolerant of these other people again fellas. Alex was growing weary of these other inmates' behavior toward his other friends. Alex hasn't been able to try to focus his attention on the person. Who is taking care of this guy's beloved pet? Joseph wasn't able to approach any of these other inmates again fellas. Alex wasn't able to be dependent upon his friend for his support during his other impactful experiences with these other inmates. Joseph was trying to figure out different ways of finishing to work on his other projects again fellas. Someone else should have been working alongside these two fugitives on their other different projects again fellas. This policeman isn't going to be able to inform these two fugitives of their current situation again, folks. This policeman can't allow these two people to try to leave the building. Unless Joseph wasn't going to be able to prove his innocence to this policeman. If Alex wasn't able to try to free his friend from his temporary confinement again fellas. Nobody else has been obligated to try to follow these other people's rules again folks. This policeman was serving these other people within his community. Because this policeman was able to grow up with them. This policeman is trying to knock on another person's door. This policeman quickly stood up on his feet again fellas. This policeman wasn't going to be able to identify any of his other suspects. Because Joseph was seeking someone else approval to gain entry into this room. This policeman was going to be opening up the door for his partner. This person was holding these two meals in the palm of his hands again fellas. This policeman was able to confirm this stuff with his supervisor. He was thinking that these two meals were for these two fugitives. "I'm going to be sitting these two trays down over there again, buddy," this policeman said. These two fugitives were able to consume their entire meals again fellas. "Okay, I'm going to be taking myself another very short time out again, buddy," this policeman said. These two fugitives were given an equal amount of time again, folks. Before these two policemen were integrating these two fugitives again fellas. "I'm not going to be allowing your cellmate to use the restroom", this policeman said. This policeman has left this integration room. This policeman was going to be returning to this specific room. These two fugitives weren't trying to respond to this policeman again fellas. These two fugitives weren't able to give these two policemen any sort of other information about their whereabouts last weekend again, fellas. So, this policeman can't try to persuade the other members of the jury to try to convict these two fugitives for these types of criminal offenses against another person, again fellas. This person wasn't assisting this policeman with his investigation again fellas. "I don't know what these two fugitives were doing on this specific night again, buddy. I'm not going to be able to try to solve this investigation of mine. someone else needs to try to address some of my other concerns for me," this policeman said. Do these two fugitives' relatives live in the same vicinity? Alex, did your friend participate in this blackmailing plot with these other people? Nobody else should have been making your friend to be explaining his other actions to them. Nobody else should have been able to use this other stuff against you. You should have been remaining silent about it again, buddy" this policeman said. Alex wasn't going to be able to respond to these two police officers' questions about this specific night again, folks. Alex has been able to vehemently deny these two policemen's accusations against him. Alex wasn't accepting responsibility for his participation in these criminal offenses with his friend. Alex has told this policeman. He has been trying to find a way of obtaining this cigarette from another person. Steve was refusing to provide this person with any of his other cigarettes again fellas. Alex has been able to depart with his friend from this vicinity again fellas. This policeman was feeling perplexed about this gentleman's question about his friend's whereabouts again, folks. Alex has been able to try to change the provision of his own story again, folks. " I'm not involved in these particular incidents with my friend. Joseph is responsible for committing this criminal offense against these other victims. I'm not going to be able to try to lie to anyone else. I didn't try to do anything else terrible to another person" Alex said. These two police officers were trying to remain skeptical of these two fugitives' stories. Alex wasn't any sort of other mere bystander again, folks. They're considering these two men as their suspects again, folks. If someone else has caught these two fugitives hacking into this agent's computer system. "If you're expecting us. If you weren't partaking in copying these computer files with him. If you didn't transfer these computer files onto another floppy disc. If I don't gather any evidence against you. You haven't shown me. You weren't attempting to blackmail this victim. If you're misleading us. If you're using this information against him. So you could've obtained some leverage against them. Hillary didn't participate in this stuff alongside you. If your goal is securing a substantial amount of money for yourselves. If they're doing your bidding for you", this policeman said. Alex was being adamant in his stance against them. Alex hasn't been providing details to them. They haven't granted them. They were given the right to speak to their lawyers. These policemen were demanding that they shouldn't vacate the building. Before they were given the chance to arrest them. This policeman has instructed them. They were placing both of these two fugitive hands behind their backs again, folks. "You're remaining in our police officer's custody today. You're speaking with this judge" this policeman said. They were placing these two fugitives in handcuffs again, folks. They're being accompanied by these two police officers. They're escorting these two fugitives to the back of the building. They're placing these two suspects into a jail cell. "I didn't expect this shit to be happening to me. They're not allowing anyone else to call their relative again, buddy," Alex said. " I'm giving those two men an opportunity to call their friends again today," this policeman said. This policeman was walking into the main lobby.

*The policeman has ordered three meals for them. (1 year)*

This chef has been making these two fugitives dinner for them. Someone else has to bring these meals to them. These two fugitives weren't sure folks, what sort of meals. They would have been eating again today. These two fugitives had to try to pick from these three different types of meals. Alex wanted to try to eat some French fries and a piece of steak for his lunch. "I'm not sure,

Alex, who is preparing my steak medium-rare for me," Joseph said. "if I'm not able to order those other detainees an expensive meal for them. I'm not sure what my partner is ordering for himself. I'm not sure if this chief can provide these other inmates with this plate of french fries and two small beverages again buddy?" Joseph said. "Maybe I'm eating this sort of meal," Alex said this stuff to them. "I'm coming right back here again buddy. I'm asking this policeman. If he can call another restaurant for me" this policeman said. This policeman has walked into a different room. This policeman was gone for at least four minutes again fellas. Whenever this policeman was returning to this room. Alex was sitting here at the moment again folks. "This person should have been on his way here again fellas. You aren't letting this chief prepare three of those meals for us" this policeman said. Alex was rubbing a small portion of his stomach again fellas. Joseph entered the room. Someone else is accompanying this creature. "I'm not sure if I'm going to be letting this guy finish using the bathroom," Ralph said. "Now I'm going to be continuing to integrate these two fugitives. Fellas, my supervisor, hasn't been able to notify me. I'm not sure if these guys' attorneys are present already again, fellas. I'm not sure if this judge has issued an arrest warrant for these two fugitives. You aren't lying to another officer of the law again, fellas. Whether I'm going to be able to assist you. I'm not making those two fugitives try to take this lie detector test again, buddy. I'm not trying to fingerprint these two fugitives. These two fugitives' attorneys should have been able to watch the surveillance footage again, fella. I'm going to be holding onto this surveillance footage for my supervisor. Until these two fugitives can speak to this judge tomorrow morning. I'm not sure if these two fugitives will be able to post their bond in the morning. I'm going to ask this judge. If I could've released these two fugitives today," this policeman said. "You shouldn't have been able to start the processing again buddy. I'm leaving the building. Because I'm looking forward to doing anything else today. I'm not going to be able to take care of this other stuff myself" Alex said. "I'm not sure if these two fugitives are feeling sorry for themselves. If I'm going to continue to try to do my investigation into this serious matter again, fellas. If I'm not going to be able to to conclude this investigation of mine. I'm not letting those fugitives leave this property," This policeman said, "If you need to try to consult with your lawyer." This policeman said this stuff to them.


## Missionary Zeal

*The policeman is getting cranky himself. (1 year)*

They haven't shown up there yet again folks. This policeman was removing these two fugitives off of their list of suspects again folks. "I'm not eating an entire meal by myself. I'm not a very patient person. Because you aren't starving me" Joseph said. "I'm not this grumpy old man," This Policeman said. Joseph isn't causing this chaos amongst these other people. Alex is getting very restless being around these other people. Alex's tummy was rumbling throughout the remainder of the whole day. Alex wasn't going to be able to overlook these other people. Because Alex wasn't able to make his other symptoms go away very rapidly again, folks. Alex was looking at this clock. These people were intriguing to this gentleman. This detective was hunting these two fugitives. They weren't returning to this specific area again folks. "I'm going to be doing this other task myself," this policeman said. Alex wasn't able to slip away from the grasp of these two policemen. Alex was going to be diverting these policemen's attention away from his friend. Alex was trying to separate from these two gentlemen. If Joseph can't pass his large turd through his colon again folks? "I'm not sure if Joseph, your turds, is going to be festering inside of you," Alex said. Alex wasn't feeling sympathetic towards anyone else. Joseph wasn't able to address his friend's situation properly again folks. "I don't have those other horses in this race. These other employers aren't going to be able to employ anyone else. I'm going to be able to adhere to these other people's demands again buddy. If I'm not going to be able to achieve these other goals of mine. I'm not becoming another very angry son of an bitch" this policeman said. Alex had been sick to his stomach again folks. " I'm a diabetic person. I don't want my blood sugar to be dropping low on me. I'm not going to be slipping into another coma again buddy. I'm not eating another one of those meals again buddy. You aren't going to have to try to transport me" Alex stated, "I'm not going to the hospital," Alex said.

## *Joseph went walking into the bathroom folks. (1 year)*

Joseph has acted inappropriately toward them. Joseph is interacting with them. He is changing his perspective about things in his life. These other people were targeting this creature. Joseph was underneath a lot of this intense scrutiny from these other people again, fellas. These other people have been able to upset this little green creature. Joseph has been able to change his demeanor around certain people. Joseph has become another devious son of an bitch. I'm not sure, folks, if something else might have befallen this gentleman. Alex didn't anticipate any of this stuff happening to his friend in the future. Joseph was going through these other long misfortunes periods again, fellas. Joseph has been referring to these other people in this derogatory manner again fellas. Joseph was leaving the room. Joseph was going to be offering his friend another chance of a lifetime. Joseph wasn't able to convince his friend to try to depend upon him. Alex isn't accepting his fate. Joseph might have conjured up his other ridiculous ideas by himself. Joseph was squatting alongside his friend. Alex couldn't step back from their situation again, fellas. Alex was feeling this wave of relief during this critical moment again fellas. Alex wasn't expecting his friend to make these other decisions for him. I'm not sure folk if Alex could have made this opportunity beneficial for himself. Alex doesn't lack any semblance of his common sense again, folks. Joseph has gone on another mission with his friend. If Joseph isn't remaining friends with this other gentleman. Joseph is feeling overjoyed with himself. Joseph might have been looking at these other prospects for himself. These two fugitives weren't getting the upper hand on their enemies. Alex's savior wouldn't have tried to offer these two guys other rare opportunities in their lives. Joseph isn't brilliant enough to see past his other insecurities again fellas. Joseph had been waiting upon his friend's arrival again, fellas. Alex is lending this alien another one of his helping hands throughout the remainder of the weekend. Joseph was approaching this gentleman. Joseph was carrying this firearm with him. Alex wasn't trying to pistol-whip his friend's enemies with this firearm. Alex isn't trying to smash another gentleman in his face with this firearm. Alex would've utilized his intellectual mind against this chum. "This person wasn't giving another person these other additional chances again today. Thus, Joseph was making this stuff impossible for these other people. I'm not going to be able to touch another gentleman's associate anytime soon again buddy. This person was trying to persuade this sheriff to terminate my employment within this office. Unless this person was trying to assault me. If this person is endangering the lives of these other people's children," Ralph said. "Okay, I'm going to try to warn them. They shouldn't have walked into the bathroom. I'm taking another huge shit in someone else toilet bowl. If anyone else is going to be able to detect another filthy aroma coming out of this bathroom. Alex, if this aroma is still lingering there in the air. You shouldn't worried about me. I'm not this major threat to your friend's lives anymore, chum. I'm not suggesting this other stuff to everyone else. You shouldn't have been hiring yourself and your roommate an escort. This person is going to try to accompany us. Maybe I was able to travel to these other places with someone else. They aren't allowing another person to try to share this room with us. I'm continuing to try to stroll into another person's lavatory," Joseph said. "Okay, if you're interested in trying to slip away from these other guests. I'm not allowing you and your other roommates to be trying to ascend out of this open window in the bathroom. I'm not letting another person try to insert both of their feet into my friend's asshole again, buddy," Ralph said. "If you're trying to unzip your pants in front of me. Because I'm having another very hard time figuring these two fugitives out again buddy. Whenever anyone else is trying to adjust their zipper on these other pants of theirs again, fella," Joseph said. "I can't get this job done properly again fella. I don't believe that this shit is in my partner's job description again, chum. I'm going to be making sure that none of these other inmates don't try to escape this place. I'm not going to be able to try to babysit anyone else anymore, chum," Ralph said. "Okay, if you're waiting out there for me. Because this bathroom is smelling like these other horses have taken another shit in there again buddy," Joseph said. "Whenever I'm trying to exit this bathroom, again chum. I'm allowing these two gentlemen to have another five minutes to themselves. If I do not grant these two fugitives any additional opportunities again, today," this policeman said, "I'm attempting to enter through the entranceway again fella." Ralph said.

## *Alex is pretending to be a crazy person. (1 year)*

The detective was furrowing up his eyebrows again, folks. Alex has these two very darting eyeballs again, folks. This policeman was presented with this evidence against them. Someone else has delivered this evidence to this policeman. Alex couldn't make any sense of this evidence again folks. Alex's lips have been pursuing the right side of his face. Joseph was rubbing his fingers against his temple. Alex was grappling with the details of this perplexing puzzle nowadays, folks. Alex's mind isn't connecting many of these other dots again fellas. Alex is trying to unravel this mystery. Alex hasn't been telling this policeman the truth about his situation again fellas. Someone else was restricting this person's pathway. Alex's face is turning these other various colors nowadays. As many of these other people. Who wasn't able to try to discourage this gentleman from moving forward with his life? "If this policeman isn't letting me and my friend use the restroom. I'm feeling my tummy is trying to explode on me. Because I'm feeling this uneasiness building up within my body again buddy. I might've shitted in my pant" Joseph said. "This policeman wasn't accompanying them. I can't depend on another person for their support during this difficult period again, buddy. I'm not able to try to communicate with another person," this policeman said. "I'm a traveler," Joseph said. "I'm not taking care of another person's pet for them," Joseph said. This policeman's supervisor hasn't given any other employees his written authorization to go through another person's belongings again, fellas. "I'm not allowing this other person to be able to bother me. I'm not following you and your roommate into a different sector. I'm trying to persuade these other employees to keep an eye on you. You can't try to leave your friend's side anytime soon again, fella," this policeman said. If they aren't interested in trying to pluck the latch off of this frame. "This policeman was trying to warn you. We're facing this danger at this very moment again buddy. You shouldn't have been doing this other shit to another person's relative" Alex said. This policeman hopped out of this armchair. This policeman fled out into the corridor. He was asking his other associate some sort of very important question about them. "I'm wondering if this judge has issued a warrant for these two fugitives' arrest again, fellas. These two fugitives weren't dealing with these other hardships again, folks. "I don't know how you're getting away with your other foolishness again, buddy," Alex said. This policeman was trying to round up them. These two policemen were pursuing them? They weren't professing their innocence to this policeman. This doctor was able to diagnose these two fugitives with some sort of other psychological disorders. They weren't placing my friend into this asylum. "This policeman wasn't going to be agreeing with you? If they are asking my other relatives about us. I'm feeling mentally unstable at this moment again buddy. I'm not going to be standing alongside you. So I'm not going to be standing trial for you. Because if you didn't try to commit an act of treason against our country. I'm not going to be lying to these other people for you. If you didn't comprehend how these people are running this judicial system in this country. You might have been trying to fuck someone else daughter" Joseph said. "I'm not receiving any sort of other messages from you. I'm going to be able to escape from this place. You're putting these other policemen in this difficult position again buddy. I wasn't able to become another distraction for you. If this policeman walked into this room. This person wasn't going to be able to design this stuff himself. I'm not going to be able to speak with my attorney. So this lawyer can defend me. Whenever I'm making an appearance in this courthouse," Alex said. Joseph was being accompanied by these two policemen. "I'm going to be able to integrate you. Whenever Joseph has been able to return to this same room. If these two fugitives were waiting to use this bathroom. Because these two fugitives were having another conversation amongst themselves. This policeman was asking this fugitive to answer these other questions for him. If this policeman wasn't holding this person and his friend personally responsible for these other crimes committed against their victims. Joseph has been hopping to both of his feet again folks. " I'm keeping another close eye on these two fugitives. I'm not letting those two guys out of my sight again tonight. I don't need these two fugitives escaping on us," this policeman said. "If Joseph isn't interested in doing some horrible things to these other people's families. I'm going to be trying to shoot a bullet in these two fugitives' directions," Ralph said.

The policeman was showing these two fugitives some pictures of themselves. (1 year)

Alex isn't responsible for them. Joseph isn't going to be cooperating with them. Joseph is an menace to society. Joseph wasn't disclosing any other information to them. These people can't prove that they have done this stuff to them. They have committed these other criminal acts against them. They do not consult with their own legal counsel again folks. before they were thrusting him and his friend into these other legal proceedings again folks. "I'm not stopping these two fugitives from seeking legal advice from an attorney. You can request this stuff from us. Alex your lawyer must be presence in this room. Whenever we're going over this evidence with you" The policeman said. Alex has been denying his own involvement in this crime against them. Alex wasn't present there at the scene again folks. "I'm not guilty of conspiring against them. Joseph was involving me and other people in this blackmailing scheme with him. Joseph was seeking potential victim again folks. So he can be targeting them. Joseph has taken this shit upon himself. " I'm needing a judges to dismiss these charges against me" Alex said. "Alex shouldn't have confess his sin to me" Joseph said. They were asking him and his friend to share their alibi with them. Alex hasn't been cooperating with them. Alex has to endure this public scrutiny again folks. Alex hasn't faltered in his assertion of his own innocence nowadays folks. They were doubtful of these two fugitive's innocence again folks. "you're not fooling anyone else again buddy" Alex said. They were obtaining the surveillance footage from this government agency. This agent has provided this policeman with a substantial amount of evidence against them. "I was given access to this surveillance video again buddy. You've done these other things during this timeframe again buddy. You've participated in these crimes with him. I've gathered statements from other specific witnesses again buddy. They can identify you" the policeman said. Alex is visibly perplexed by it again folks. Alex is struggling to comprehend this shit again folks. Alex does know how they're able to gather this evidence against them. Alex was rubbing his hair again folks. "Alex has been avoiding another court trial. the police officer isn't going to show these two fugitives any compassion again folks. "I'm leaving this shit in god hands again buddy," Joseph said. They're displaying the crime scene photos again folks. Alex wasn't concealing his lack of enthusiasm again folks. Whenever they're claiming that they have gathered this evidence against them. Alex acknowledged that he had a birthmark on his upper body again folks. Alex denies that there isn't any resemblance between them. They're been comparing these guys' sizes again folks. "If you're not able to tell the difference between them and us," Alex said. "If you're lying to me. I'm not going to believe you" the policeman said. They share the same characteristics as them. "I'm visiting my mom at a nursing home," Alex said. They presented this man with his mother's death certificate. Alex hasn't been able to persuade them. Another woman has been impersonating his deceased mother. " I'm getting in touch with an employee. I asked the nurse. If she is verifying the story. I'm getting to the bottom of it again buddy" the policeman said. " If you do get ahold of a nurse for me. They're going to confirm these details with you. They mistakenly provided the police officer with an incorrect birth certificate belonging to this guy's grandmother. "If you're pursuing this matter further again buddy. If you're looking for information about me" Alex said. "I'll contact an employer of the county clerk's office. I'm going to request this person give you, and your friend a copy of my mother's death certificates today. They would've kept a copy of every person's death certificate in this person's office. So if you haven't provided me and my friend with some accurate information about your mom's death again buddy" this policeman said. They're going to charge them with obstruction of justice. Whenever they've deliberately obstructed the law enforcement officer duties again folks. "I'm not forcing someone else to take a lie detector test for me," the policeman said. "I'm not able to test you. Because buddy it is preventing me, and my friend from practicing our religion. Buddy the preacher wouldn't allow it. Because they don't believe in the accuracy of these tests again buddy" Joseph said.

## Forcing Power

*Joseph was being a smartass towards his friend. (1 year)*

Whenever this guy was pulling his vehicle into the parking lot. Nobody else was expecting these two policemen to be there on the scene. These two fugitives were hearing the sound of those two policemen patrol cars' again fellas. Alex was feeling a little tense about someone else again fellas. Whenever these two policemen were stepping out of their cars. As they were heading their way into the building. Everyone else wasn't going to be able to try to help these two fugitives. Because Alex was facing judgment for participating in many of these other criminal activities with his friend. Joseph has been able to anticipate this stuff happening to themselves. Whenever the policeman was opening up both sides of his vehicle. This policeman was able to extract both of those gentlemen from the rear of their patrol cars. Everyone else could hear the sound of those four gentlemen's footsteps echoing across the payment. These policemen were able to get a confession from these two fugitives. These policemen were moving those two misfits into an integration room. The cop wasn't going to become accommodating to these two fugitives. "You can have a seat over there again fellows," this policeman said. This policeman is placing these sets of handcuffs around their suspect's wrists again, fellas. This policeman was trying to restrict these two fugitives' movements again today. This patrolman was going to be resting alongside these two fugitives. This policeman wasn't going to be approaching any of these other fugitives anytime soon again, fellas. This policeman has to get his partner to deliver this message to them. Joseph doesn't understand the importance of this policeman's investigation again fellas. This policeman was going over the process with them. This policeman was going to be able to guide these two fugitives through some of these other legal proceedings again, fellas. This policeman was trying to conduct his ongoing investigation into these two fugitives' criminal offenses throughout the remainder of the day. Because these two fugitives have been able to commit many of their crimes against these other Victims. They weren't going to be able to trust this policeman with their livelihood. They weren't going to be able to reach any sort of agreement with these two policemen. "Okay, I'm telling you. But I am required to make every single person understand this stuff at any particular moment again fellas. So I'm reading this document to you. I'm not sure what this guy's name is again, fellas," the policeman said. "Buddy my name is Alex Jones," Alex said. Joseph wasn't able to try to decline those two policemen's requests again fellas. This policeman was able to get this creature to provide his actual first name to him. Joseph is this remarkably stubborn creature. Joseph was displaying his other narcissistic ways to these two policemen. Joseph wasn't threatened by these two policemen's authority over him. Because Joseph doesn't have to try to respond to any of those other policeman's questions about himself. Joseph was encompassing both of his two lips together. Nobody else has been able to prepare this creature for this ongoing miscarriage of justice again fellas. "You should have known, Buddy, that my first name is Joseph Flanagan," Joseph said. They are going to need to try to provide this policeman with their current addresses again fellas. Joseph has been able to withhold information from them. "Okay, If you're going to be refusing to speak to me. I'm not allowing these two fugitives to be communicating with both of their attorneys. You will be pleading your entire case to some judge. You're going to be talking to this judge about this stuff again, fellas," This Policeman said. Alex wasn't able to try to navigate his way out of this situation again fellas. Because they are facing these other types of legal predicaments at this moment again fellas. This lawyer is going to be able to provide those two fugitives with his other legal expertise on this legal matter again, folks. Alex wasn't able to comment on his other strategies during this transitional moment again fellas. Folks If these two fugitives are waiting to see their counselor present there with them. So these two lawyer can try to instruct their client.

Whenever these two fugitives should try to respond to this policeman. This attorney should know how he should try to walk his client through this delicate process again fellas. Even most of these other inmates were given the option to try to speak to their lawyers on many different occasions. If these two fugitives don't understand the following indictment against themselves? These two fugitives were being charged with violating these other laws within a certain timeframe. " Yes, this gentleman's mom is sucking on another person's penis again fella. I'm trying to inseminate with this policeman's relative again fellas. This woman is giving birth to this descendant of mine. This person shouldn't have been able to inhale upon my long phalluses again, fella," Joseph said. "I'm asking these two fugitives. If these two fugitives know why anyone else would have tried to steal these several documents with their counterparts again fellas?" the policeman said. "I'm not sure if I know Alex, the answer to this policeman question again, fellas. I wasn't in this area" Joseph said. "Nobody else was able to provide me and my partner with an actual description of our two suspects. I'm not sure if you were at the crime scene. " I'm not sure if I was sitting here with this gentleman's mother. This doctor was able to help my mother to try to restore her life, buddy," Alex remarked. "I'm not letting anyone else be making these other sick jokes at these other people's expense again, fella. I have been speaking with many of your other relatives about your other criminal activities again buddy. this woman isn't considered dead to anyone else again, buddy. I don't know why you're interested in trying to steal these other important documents from this government facility. You weren't able to try to blackmail another person. You weren't trying to use this other stuff against them. You weren't gaining some sort of other leverage against many of your other victims," the policeman said. "I'm going to be trying to shut my partner's big fat mouth for him. I'm not trying to incriminate myself" Alex said. "Okay, I'm not sure if I know Where you were on this particular night. Because If you were hacking into an agent's account again fellow? I have been able to speak with these other different people about you. This guy has been trying to inform us. You weren't going to make able to provoke him" the police officer stated.

## *Joseph was making a fool of himself. (1 year)*

Joseph is telling them. They should've known something else about another certain subject again, folks. Joseph is worried these other people are trying to defame them. Alex has found this shit very puzzling to everyone else. Alex didn't tolerate someone else making these other insulting comments towards these other people. Joseph was trying to insult many of these other people's relatives. These other people weren't finding this creature's jokes amusing to them. Joseph has been waiting to follow through with his other career aspirations again folks. These other people shouldn't have been trying to hinder their own children's lives. These other people weren't allowing their children to try to explore their sexuality with the opposite genders. I'm not sure if this stuff is getting difficult for these two fugitives. Chelsea is struggling with this concept that there is another supernatural being again fellas. Who has the authority to try to control the weather conditions on this planet? I'm not sure if this shit is uncommon for everyone else. If these other people aren't going to be questioning our Savior about their children's existence in this world. "I'm not going to be ridiculing another person for trying to make their own decisions in this timeframe again sweetheart. I'm not trying to acknowledge another person's dreams again, sweetheart. Because these other people don't try to acknowledge me and my dreams again sweetheart. I haven't received any of those other details about this specific person. I'm not relating this stuff to anyone else lives" this guy said. Joseph maintained that he had these other spiritual beliefs again fellas. Alex was going to be working alongside these other people. This guy is this nightclub owner. John was making these other derogatory comments about this young lady's promiscuous again folks. Joseph was comparing another young lady's breasts to another very large flotation device again folks. Joseph was trying to inform another person to be charging these other people for staying there with them. Joseph has been trying to approach these other people. Because Joseph wants to hire these other escorts to try to fuck him and his roommate. Joseph wasn't able to disagree with another person. What these other people were saying about them? Joseph is blaming this escort for letting another person try to remove her clothing for her again, folks. Joseph is getting another chance to be fucking with this escort. Joseph is establishing another personal connection with these other escorts. Joseph is feeling confused about these other people's dismissiveness towards himself and his roommate. Alex wasn't being employed by many of these other escorting companies. I'm not sure if this stuff would've been very beneficial for everyone else. They weren't capable of rewarding anyone else. Alex wasn't losing his virginity to these other women. Chelsea could have changed another small portion of her boyfriend's life. Joseph hasn't been trying to respond to anyone else. Joseph doesn't know why these people were able to try to pursue many of these other professions. Joseph has been describing this shit to everyone else. Chelsea's breasts are looking very saggy to everyone else. Alex wasn't able to be disappointed in his mother's other choice in his lifetime. Alex wasn't thinking about any of these other specific topics at this very moment of the day. If this woman is taking off another small portion of these other articles of clothing for these gentlemen to try to pay her for most of her other services. "I'm not trying to flog you or anyone else," Alex said. Alex isn't trying to reprimand another person's wife for her behavior toward someone else. Alex wasn't engaging in these other sexual encounters with these other women. These other escorts weren't able to seek other employment opportunities within these other reputable escort companies. Joseph wasn't occupying these other escorts' minds. If Joseph weren't interested in doing this other shit to these other escorts. Chelsea wasn't interested in planting both of her palms onto those two fugitive's penises again folks. "I'm not using this stuff against anyone else. I'm not some very vicious animal. But I'm not hitting anyone else over their head with this very large pool stick again buddy. If they weren't upsetting me," the policeman uttered this stuff underneath his breaths again folks. "I'm not going to be fixing this problem between them," Alex said. "If I'm using this gadget myself. I'm not sure if Buddy this crap is bothering them. Chelsea is causing distractions among them. Chelsea is going to be flirting with them. She was exposing her two very large breasts to them. If they aren't clutching onto this young lady's nipples again, buddy," Joseph said. This detective is becoming discouraging to them. They weren't capable of placing two of those fugitives in shackles. They were attempting to shove these two fugitives into the passenger seat of their car. "If you aren't capable of warning them. I'm not settling these other disputes between us. They aren't forcing my friend to testify against me. I'm not in another pleasant mood again today" Alex said. This detective has slammed the door shut behind them. This police officer did climb into his partner's automobile. "I'm not recommending your friend to seek another good therapist. I'm not dealing with your friend's anger problems again chum. If you're going to be interrupting me. I'm using this canister of Maze on them. I'm going to be spraying your friends with this chemical." This policeman said this stuff to them. "I'm not glancing at someone else parents' picture again buddy. I'm not hoping out of this guy's automobile window. Because I do not have these other scary hallucinations again, buddy. If they weren't forcing someone else to look at them" Joseph said. Alex was sitting upon his Perch. Alex wasn't talking to any of them.

### *A policeman has apprehended them. (1 year)*

This clerk was retrieving his cell phone from his other jacket pocket. This clerk was using this stuff against these two fugitives. The clerk has been seeking the help of this police officer again, folks. This clerk is expressing his different grievances with this policeman. The clerk is dialing the number to this police precinct. Whenever this operator has been able to respond to this gentleman's emergency. This guy was sharing his version of his emergency with this operator. This operator was trying to assist this other caller with their emergency. This clerk was describing these two fugitive disruptive behaviors towards these other customers. The clerk provided this operator with a vague description of these two suspects. The policeman was advising this person not to take any sort of action against these two perpetrators. This policeman wasn't trying to encourage another person to take the law into their hands again, fellas. "I'm not going to be able to obstruct those fugitive pathways", this clerk said. This person was trying to prevent those individuals from exiting through this exit of the building. Alex was trying to avoid these other customers. Joseph wasn't expecting those police officers to try to capture him. Alex was causing another disturbance amongst themselves. Alex was getting very frustrated with himself. Alex has been attempting to try to bribe this individual. "You aren't making my friend lose his temper with anyone else," Joseph said. Alex was going to try to punch another customer in his face again, folks. This clerk was utilizing many of his different skills on them. The clerk didn't acquire his other set of skills through these other different methods again, folks. This assassin has been able to put this person through these other tedious training sessions. "If you aren't capable of trying to defend yourself. Whenever someone else is trying to assault you", this clerk said. The clerk is actively working against these two fugitives. He is trying to ensure these other people's safety again, folks. If this clerk isn't interested in apprehending these two fugitives. This clerk might have prevented another person from being injured by both of these two fugitives. These other employees were prohibited from trying to physically harm another person. "I'm an employee," this clerk said. The clerk wasn't able to benefit from this shit himself. The clerk couldn't do anything else to these two fugitives. The clerk has to try to remove these other customers from this equation again fellas. So the clerk isn't handling this situation between himself and these two fugitives. "I haven't gotten any sort of other life insurance policy again buddy," this clerk said. The customer was unable to avoid these two fugitives. This customer has fallen to the floor. Before these other customers were trying to intervene on this young man's behalf again, folks. Joseph has been inflicting pain upon this other customer. This clerk is expecting those policemen to show up there again today. Whenever they were arriving at the scene of the crime. They were climbing out of their patrol car. Before they were able to remove those two people from the property. These two policemen were going to be conducting a thorough search of this owner's property. This policeman was trying to search through those two individuals' pants pockets. If Joseph was able to conceal any other potential weapons upon himself. This policeman would have taken these two fugitives into his custody. They are reading those people their rights to remain silent again, folks. "I'm going to be thinking about me and my partner transporting these two fugitives to our jailhouse," this Policeman said. "I haven't gotten any other weapon on me," Alex said. "I'm going to be able to strip-search these two fugitives," this policeman said. "I'm referring to another person's pussy as this stinky little hole again buddy. She hasn't killed anyone else. Whenever this gentleman was trying to force me and someone else to eat this young lady's pussy for her again, buddy", Joseph said.

*Joseph wasn't trying to use a couple of his own brain cells again fellows. (1 year)*

Alex has been able to use his amazing ability to get everything else from his other friends. Alex was being observant of his other surroundings again, folks. Alex saw those other items resting on this bookshelf. John was able to scatter these other items across the floor. Alex was going to be able to reciprocate these other favors to his friend. Alex was picking up these other items for himself. Alex was tossing those same other items back at his friend's face again fellas. Alex was able to try to avoid getting struck in his mouth by those other items again folks. Alex was defending himself. Joseph isn't the creator. "I'm not going to be getting into touch with these other people. These other people seem to be ridiculous to me," this customer said. Alex has been able to persuade most of these other people not to throw away these other small objects again, folks. Alex has been very cautious of his friend. Joseph wasn't able to start criticizing many of these other people for believing in our Savior. Joseph is insulting these other people's spiritual beliefs. Joseph has been trying to ignore them. "If you aren't leaving these other customers alone again buddy. Someone else is trying to rearrange your friend's face for him," Alex said. Alex had to try to remain calm for a while again, folks. Joseph isn't regretting this stuff that he has done to everyone else. Joseph doesn't need to agree with everyone else opinion of them. "I'm not sure why you're acting in such another peculiar manner again, buddy. If you don't have any of these other brain cells left inside of your skull. If you aren't willing to use your brain cells again buddy. You're going to be ending up in this other position again, buddy," Alex said. Joseph wasn't going to be able to approach anyone else. "If you're going to be snitching on someone else. I'm going to be able to cast another spell on you. I'm going to be able to develop many of my other skills within another short amount of time again buddy. I'm not this very magical elf" Joseph said. Joseph, you can't try to place another hex on these other people? Alex was trying to shrug off this other stuff again folks. Joseph's eyes have been rolling into the back of his skull. Joseph was speaking with them. He was using this ominous chant to convey his message to these other people again folks. "I'm not feeling comfortable with anyone else. I'm not going to be afraid of these other people" this customer said. Alex was slapping this alien on both sides of his shoulder blades. "You are an idiot to everyone else. If someone else is going to be able to walk in here on us" Alex said. These other people could have these other fugitives committed to these other insane asylums.

## Trial and Turmoil

*Joseph doesn't know, if he should try to behave himself (1 year)*

Alex was shocked at his friend's rudeness towards other people. Alex has been guiding them. He wants everyone to adjust their conduct around certain people. Joseph is interacting with them. Joseph is unsure of himself. How can this guy initiate a conversation with this young lady? He is at a loss for words again folks. whenever Joseph is speaking to this young lady. this young lady may possess a highly delicate disposition again folks. Joseph is interested in this young lady again folks. Joseph wants to take steps toward this young lady. So they can build a stronger connection between themselves. But this lady has explicitly prohibited anyone else from contacting her family. The young lady deliberately ignores him. The young lady has declined this guy's offers again folks. They want to sleep with this young lady. this young lady is avoiding them. Joseph persistently attempts to keep flirting with this young lady. The young lady has threatened them. She is going to take some legal action against them. Because they are harassing this young lady again folks. they must make these two fugitives face the consequences for their actions again folks. Alex firmly believes that they should give these two fugitives a second chance to redeem themselves. everyone has the potential to redeem themselves. They deserve an opportunity again folks. So they can do so in my opinion again folks. "I haven't been observing them," Alex said. Joseph can't change this young lady's opinion of him. The clerk is uncertain about them. he provides the two fugitives the opportunity to exit the store. The clerk is reprimanding them. Folks it would've been very helpful to him. The clerk is trying to establish communication with an employee of the police department. The clerk has given this operator instructions to send a policeman to this location. The clerk has been patiently waiting for them. So they can escort these two individuals off of their property again folks. Joseph is curious whether this guy's mother has breastfed him. This individual's mother has an unpleasant nature again folks. If this woman is fucking these men again folks. "I'm betting you. This lady is performing oral sex on them. This lady might've been placing this guy's engorged penis in her mouth again buddy?" Joseph said. Joseph does lack restraint again folks. whenever Joseph is discussing this lady's promiscuity with someone else again folks. "You mustn't have done this shit yourself," Alex said. Alex is feeling upset again folks. Alex is trying to convince them. Because Alex wants to join their orgy again folks. After they leave this area again folks. This young lady is spending time with them. She enjoys these men's company again folks. Joseph has based his opinion on other things again folks. This young lady has been fucking a lot of these people. Whoever is in this young lady's social circle again folks. "If this lady doesn't want to fuck them," Alex said. Joseph has developed this strong belief in himself. this young lady has been engaging in these other sexual acts with them. This young lady wants to exchange sexual favors for these men to offer her financial support again folks. whoever offered this young lady the highest amount of compensation for her services again folks. this woman is a crack whore. this individual has refused to criticize his mother's shitty behavior again folks. Alex is unsure of the reasons behind this guy's decision again folks. Joseph is left wondering if this guy has a motivation again folks. Alex has been grabbing ahold of this alien's shirt sleeve again folks. Alex is forcing this creature to accompany him. The clerk is punching the creature in the face again folks. Folks this shit is due to this creature making these other derogatory comments about his mother. "I'm a very nice person. But they're getting on my damn nerves again folks. Because they're a little annoying to me" this clerk said. " I'm not putting up with those guys' shenanigans anymore again folks," this customer said. They've encountered them. Folks this poster features the distinct likenesses of themselves. Many of those store owners in the area again folks. They've been placing these guys' wanted posters in their store windows. They're a couple of idiots to them. These two individuals lack the fundamental understanding again folks. I think that this person can't construct a coherent sentence himself. Alex is concerned that the presence of a policeman could potentially lead to trouble for them. They would be sent to jail for a very long time folks. They have decided that they must try to flee the area right away folks. So whenever these two policemen arrived at the scene of the crime again folks. The clerk has provided a detailed explanation of the situation to the policeman. I think that this clerk has included a description of these two fugitives' facial features again folks. The clerk has expressed his grievance with them. "they were making a nuance of themselves" this clerk said. The policeman has been diligently searching for the two fugitives. The policeman has advised the clerk to personally protect the owner's investment. The clerk is assisting the policeman in apprehending the suspect. " If this guy is lying to me. If you didn't see, which direction of the city. they might have been headed in right now buddy?" This policeman said. The policeman is currently engaged in an investigation into a separate crime against folks. He is diligently pursuing leads that someone else has provided him. "If we have made an error in judgment ourselves. After I have tried to collect most of this other evidence myself. If I can't prove that these two fugitives were responsible for committing this crime again buddy. I might have to dismiss these charges that were brought against the two of them" the first policeman said. " I do believe that those other two guys look exactly like them," this clerk said. This clerk did try to apprehend them. But they got away themselves. Because Joseph was trying to throw this stuff at them. I believe that it was a little earlier ladies and gentlemen.

## *Joseph saw that there was this shop himself. (1 year)*

Whenever Joseph's has placed both of his own feet upon the asphalt. Alex was walking two inches behind him. Folks there was this small market. Whenever Joseph saw it from distance folks. They went strolling into this shop folks. "So I'm trying to acquire some of these other separate items for myself. I can't understand that why we're stranded on this airplane awhile again chum" Joseph said. "If you're going to cause some sort of disruption yourself. If I don't agree with you. If I don't want to go through with this crap again buddy. I'm wishing that I could've gone in there with you. You better not provoke any of them. Because they might try to consider the two of us. Joseph an couple of these other outcasts buddy" Alex said. Whenever they went walking into the shop. Joseph was shuffling both of his own feet towards this store's candy aisle folks. Joseph was determined to try to search through a couple of these other items again folks. They had put some of this stuff on a shelf. So they can try to display it for some of their own customers. Joseph would've preferred to be able to choose for himself. Which of these other two items that he would've prefer to purchase for himself. Josephs would've preferred to be able to choose the item that he would've loved to try to eat in the first place again folks. Because Joseph thought that this candy did look very appealing to him. If Joseph could've savored this special occasion again folks. Whenever he tried to place a single morsel of those food into his own mouth today folks. Alex was running toward an totally different aisle of the store again folks. I've believed that Alex saw that there is another woman. Who was shouting at her own friend again folks. I'm wondering, if Joseph did try to do some of these other hideous things to her chums? If they were having an exchange of remarks and ladies and gentlemen if it were about themselves. Alex was feeling completely puzzled by it again ladies and gentlemen. Alex was determined that he wanted to figure out, what this foolishness was about himself. So he decided to approach them. " If this female could describe to me. Why she felt the need to shout at a roommate of mine? Did Joseph do some dreadful thing to you. Lady excuses him. This critter possesses some inner conflicts that he must seek to work out himself. I would encourage my roommate to seek a psychiatrist. Who can prescribe my friend a medication that he could take himself. I believe this medication would help him" Alex said. " You shouldn't get embroiled in this crap yourself. Alex, whenever this foolishness doesn't bother you. I chose to plead with her. If this lady would hand over her telephone number to me" Joesph said. "I think this critter sought to snag me. If you wished to make your friend leave this store. The guy is bothering me. I think this critter has made some harsh statements about me. This creature called women bosoms as two large milk dispenser buddy" The lady said. Alex is perturbed with his roommate behavior toward women in general people. This critter was an inconvenience for him. " If you don't quit doing these things to this woman. If I continue to intercede on the side of this female. You're not a predator. Who is seeking to feed on its prey chum" Alex said. " I'm making an effort to speak to the salesperson myself. I'll inform the clerk that this critter is seeking to pester me" the lady said. Joseph was seeking to coax this woman himself. This lady mustn't reveal everything that this critter has said to her chums. Especially to the salesperson. Because Joseph doesn't want another human causing an disturbance within the store chums. Joseph sought to persuade this individual himself. He wouldn't do it to another guy wife himself. If this youthful female would give this critter another moment to rehabilitate himself, " I'm going to behave myself" Joesph said. This female determined that, she would continue to run to a particular area of the store. So this woman could remove herself. Because people it was becoming an inhospitable climate for her chums. This female greeted this salesperson. This lady was continuing to mention this crap to this clerk. What this critter done to her today chums. If this salesperson wished to warn someone else. Who works at the police bureau? " they will place us in jail chum" Alex said. The clerk wasn't happy with these two customers himself. The clerk came walking towards them. They can't afford to lose any of their customer's fellows. Because people of these two gentlemen' wrongdoings todays.  This gentleman has directed these two fellows to leave the store. Before, he seeks to get in contact with a detective from a police department. "If I have to influence a detective to come here today chums.  So he could accompany these two gentlemen from the construction" the shop clerk said. " I don't believe that you will do it yourself.  You don't have any courage yourself" Joesph said.

## *Steve wanted to search their room (2 years)*

" I don't know anything else about them. I'm not trying to copy any of these people's documents again buddy. But I'm telling you. If I'm finding out these other things about you. You're not the ones. Who had someone to copy those documents for you? I'm telling you. I'm going to be returning here soon again buddy. I'm going to be reminding you. I'm thinking about hiring someone. Who can dust the computer keyboard for me? I'm thinking about searching for your and your friend's fingerprints again buddy. I want to get someone else to make an impression of these two fugitives' fingerprints for me. I'm going to be sending your two guys' fingerprints to our forensic lab again fellows. So this lab technician can do his analysis on your guy's fingerprints for me. Whenever this lab technician enters your two guy's fingerprints into our agency database fellows. I'm hoping that this technician is going to be able to match your fingerprints to our suspect fingerprints again buddy. So whenever I do receive the lab technician report again buddy. So whenever I receive this person's report again buddy. I'm going to read this person's report thoroughly for myself. Then I'm taking an impression of your two guys' fingerprints for myself. I'm thinking about making sure that you're not going to be getting away with anything else again buddy. If Alex this person's report does confirm my suspicion about you and your friend's involvement in this other criminal offense again buddy. I'm going to be locking you and your friend up in jail for a very long time again buddy. I'm going to be making sure that someone is going to be getting this stuff done for me. So if you want to know if I'm allowing someone else to search through your belongings again buddy" Steve said. "I'm not letting anyone else do anything to me. If you're not getting a search warrant from a judge again buddy. We do have the right to defend ourselves. I'm thinking about getting someone to prevent you and your partner from doing these other unlawful searches around this place again buddy. So I'm going to be suggesting that you shouldn't have someone else searching through our belongings again buddy. Unless you want me and my friend to go file a lawsuit against your police department again buddy. I do know something else about these laws in this state. I'm going to be working on it again buddy. You can't just search someone's else premises without having probable cause to do so again buddy. You're not allowed to search this room again buddy" Alex said. "I'm getting myself and my partner a search warrant from a judge again buddy. You can believe it again buddy. If someone else does come across these documents on your premises again buddy. I'm arresting you and your roommate on suspicion of being a part of a criminal organization again buddy. You're going to be going to prison again buddy. you're not going to be seeing the sunset again buddy?" Steven said.

## *Alex was trying to insult another individual himself. (2 years)*

Alex was trying to make his interpretation of his friend's life. Alex was picking out these different aspects of his friend's lifestyle. He wasn't going to be able to accept his friend's choices in his lifestyle. Alex wasn't interested in trying to mimic anything else in his friend's lifestyle. Alex was trying to incorporate some of these other things into his lifestyle. Alex has been making some of these other excellent choices for himself. Whenever this person is sitting behind this very large desk. Alex has been waiting to try to approach this gentleman. But they were conversing amongst each other again fellas. Hillary isn't interested in keeping many of her other romantic affairs with these other gentlemen a secret from her husband. "I'm not going to be looking forward to me and my partner trying to hook up with another person's wife? Because I'm not doing these other nasty things with this lady's daughter. We weren't interested in learning about the same things again fella. I'm going to be able to search the globe. I'm going to be searching for another specific type of woman. So I can try to climb alongside these other women in the bed. This person must have been an identical twin to someone like Selina Gomez. Because I'm getting much older than my other friends again fella. I'm not trying to fuck another individual. If this person doesn't possess any types of other skills again buddy. If this person weren't going to be able to perform these other things on me. If Hillary is trying to advance her political career within this specific era. Hillary isn't interested in trying to solve her other emotional problems for herself. I'm trying to inflict a lesser amount of pain upon everyone else. If I'm not going to be able to fold another person's body in half again, buddy. I'm not going to be performing any other type of sexual activity on these other women. If I'm not able to try to turn someone else into some other useless object again, buddy. I'm not going to be able to play with any of these other women's breasts at this exact moment again, buddy. Hillary doesn't have this worn-out type of body again, buddy. If Hillary isn't interested in moving around in the bedroom. Hillary doesn't have to speak to me. While I'm trying to fuck this lady in her asshole," Joseph said. This person was shouting at them. "You must have known this stuff about my spouse again fellows. I'm not going to be able to introduce someone else to my wife. Becky isn't out shopping with another person. Becky is trying to search for other household supplies," this gentleman said. Alex was looking into this guy's eye sockets again fellas. "You shouldn't have taken this shit upon yourself. So you're making these other unsavory remarks about my wife's breast size again, fellas," this guy said. "You better try to prepare your friend. Because I'm going to be trying to kick your friend's ass for him. I'm not trying to persuade another person to call a taxi cab company. You're going to be getting your friend in trouble with these policemen. You aren't getting yourself and your friend involved in this situation between the two of us? Buddy whenever I'm not sure buddy if this shit should have stayed between both of us. You shouldn't have tried to get into contact with these other people. So, I'm trying to relax my two aching feet on this couch for a while again fella. I'm going to be able to enjoy myself. You shouldn't have gotten my friend arrested by these two policemen" Joseph said.

3

# Chapter 3 Between Madness and Meaning

## Escape Plans and Paranoia

*When Alex has gone to the airport. Joseph was trying to watch a porn video. (5 years)*

Alex is currently evacuating this sector. Alex went back to the compartment. Alex was going to be using this car. Alex reserved two aircraft seats for themselves. Alex was sitting in one of those seats again, folks. They aren't allowing these two people to climb abroad of the aircraft. If Alex doesn't have a ticket in his hands again, folks. I'm not sure if this shit would've been impossible for someone else to be traveling abroad on an aircraft. If they were going to be flying overseas. Alex was very unenthusiastic about his upcoming trip to the country of Russia. Joseph shouldn't have been following his friend's advice again, folks. Alex should've stayed in touch with his friends. Alex was going to be given his friend some of his guidance again folks. Joseph shouldn't have been allowed to engage in this other person's foolishness again, folks. While Alex is standing at the airport. Alex was going to be buying those supplies again fellas. Alex wants to purchase a disguise for themselves. Because Alex is going to be ensuring a portion of his identity remains hidden from the public sector. Alex is going to be proceeding with his other purchases again folks. Alex is purchasing those other personal items or himself. Alex has been contemplating this stuff every day. Joseph can try to handle his other problems himself. Because Alex requires someone else's assistance again, folks. "We're going to be handling our problems ourselves," Alex said. Alex is going to remain steadfast this time again, folks. If you don't try to inform me. Before you're getting ready to flee this area. I'm not doing it by myself" Joseph said. Alex was worried about how this stuff might have been affecting his friendship with him. Alex was considering an alternative means of transportation again, folks. So Alex can be traveling to the hospital. If there is another emergency. If they weren't going to be reminding him. Joseph is avoiding facing these other various challenges during his friend's absence again, folks. Joseph has been feeling his anxiety mounting during this period again folks. Alex is going to be dreading someone else apprehending him. What If they're going to get seriously injured again, fellas? Alex has taken this stuff upon himself. Because Alex has been given the unfortunate task of sorting through this drama again fellas. They aren't going to be taking this other stuff lightly again fellas. Joseph is curious about their travel plans again folks. If they're going to be flying across the world. "I'm going to be collecting many of my other personal belongings again, buddy," Joseph said. Joseph has been indulging in his friend's other fantasies again, folks. Joseph wants to try to receive some oral pleasure from this escort. Alex wasn't sure if this stuff had the potential to significantly improve their lives. Joseph is experiencing this other difficulty whenever he is trying to maintain his erection again, folks. Joseph is becoming skeptical of seeing a therapist for his sexuality again, folks. "I'm not going to be feeling nervous about it again, buddy," Joseph said. Joseph is going to be willing to contribute his money towards their expenses again, folks. If Joseph can't pay this escort for her other services. "I'm not going to be hiring an escort," Alex said. Joseph is trying to avoid paying this escort's other exorbitant fee again, folks. Because Joseph lacks the funds to cover this lady's other expenses again, folks. "I'm going to be relaxing a little more frequently again, buddy. If I'm not going to be focusing on myself" Alex said. "I don't know how we are exactly alike again, buddy?" Joseph replied to his friend. These other people don't understand it again fellas. Whenever someone else does something, e, else fo,r everyone else voluntarily again, fellas. I'm not sure if someone else should have this level-headed mindset. Joseph has been carefully considering the disadvantages of being born in another woman's body again fellas. Joseph has come to this conclusion about these other people's professions again, folks. If they weren't interested in declining to provide their other client with these types of services again folks. Joseph doesn't want this escort to be rejecting him. Joseph is specifically seeking a one-night stand with someone else again folks. Whenever they're giving another job again folks. Joseph is going to be embarrassing his friend. Joseph doesn't disclose this information to anyone else. He has erectile dysfunction again fellas. "I'm going to be relieving some of this stress myself. Because I'm going to be having these other unnatural urges in my life again, buddy," Joseph said. "If you're going to be coping with another male sexuality problem again, buddy. Because if you're going to be experiencing these other symptoms again fellas. If you're going to allow me. I'm not sure if this shit isn't too important to me. I don't agree with everyone else. Because you're making this situation a little complicated again buddy. If this woman is going to be accommodating your friend's needs again buddy. you're going to be fulfilling your friend's other sexual appetites again buddy? if you're getting another person to be participating with you. Whenever you're having these other sick sexual fantasies of sleeping with another person? this young woman could've enjoyed it again, fella," Alex said. Joseph has been trying to inform his friend. Alex wouldn't know how he should try to handle his friend's emotional outburst again folks. if Joseph isn't getting to engage in another sexual encounter with the escort. As he was going to be expressing many of his other frustrations with his friend again, folks. "You don't know what this shit is going to be like for me. whenever you haven't been going through this shit yourself. I'm going to be having this other stress building up inside of me. I'm going to be trying to reduce some of these symptoms of mine. If this lady doesn't agree to be performing oral sex on me. I'm going to be trying to persuade this lady to bend down on both of her knees again fella. So this escort can perform another decent blow job on me. I'm going to be requesting to have this young lady place a percentage of her large head in between my pelvis area. Because I'm fixing another dilemma of mine. I'm not going to be suppressing many of these other sexual urges of mine. If I'm continuing to have these types of sexually explicit dreams about another human being. Maybe I'm going to be easing most of this tension between us. I have been given the right to express myself. God is going to be watching over me. So I'm not just another citizen. If an escort does try to offer another person a piece of this young lady's pussy in the future. I'm not going to be turning this lady's proposal down again buddy. you shouldn't have to agree with this very crude statement of mine. If you're going to be trying to fuck another person. What if this woman is going to be in complete denial again, buddy? What if this lady is going to refuse to engage in intercourse with us? What if this woman doesn't know how to last more than an hour again, buddy?What if a policeman would've caught us? Then this judge would have tried to send us. somewhere to another maximum prison. What If this young lady doesn't want to fuck another person. What If we're not getting another opportunity to have sex with another person? I'm not sure if this stuff won't be another good idea again buddy. If we shouldn't have done this shit to these other people" Joseph said. "I'm not sure that there is no way in hell. you're going to be able to pull this stuff off again, fella. I shouldn't have approved of any of it again fella. you're going to be using someone else hard-earned money for yourself. You're going to be losing your fucking mind? this lady isn't going to be willing to have sex with an alien. She would have freaked out about it right now. This woman wouldn't have let another alien go near her very delicious-tasting pussy, in my opinion, again, fella. They would have been trying to send someone else again. I think that they would have been sending you or another alien to some other kind of scientific lab where they would have been conducting some kind of those other weird science experiments. " No, I would have preferred to do this shit to anything else again, buddy. This scientist isn't going to be sticking some sharp object inside of my friend's asshole, in my opinion, again, buddy. What If this young lady is going to try to fondle me? I'm not sure if I'm going to be sticking some type of foreign object inside of another woman's asshole. I'm not sure if many of those other ladies are going to be sticking these objects in a small alien penis again, buddy. I'm not sure what this other stuff is being called again buddy. I could have made this young lady's heart beat a little faster again, buddy. If I would've been given the opportunity again buddy. If this young lady is waiting to experience this pleasurable moment for herself. what it is like again buddy. Whenever an alien is trying to stick a large percentage of his penis inside of this young lady's uterus again, buddy. You might've had a very small penis again buddy. I'm not going to be comparing my penis to his penis again fella. Joseph has a very tiny penis again fella. this young woman should have known better, in my opinion again, buddy. If this young lady doesn't know how to use another person's penis to pleasure herself. I don't know, the person. who would have shown this woman? how to use another person's penis properly, in my opinion again, buddy. Maybe this young lady would have been liking to suck on another massive male penis, in my opinion, again, buddy.

## *Alex believed that so many of those other democrats were corrupt politicians. (5 years)*

They have affected him. Alex has been able to convinced himself. Alex wasn't capable of stopping them. They weren't capable of achieving many of their dreams again folks. Furthermore, Alex was engaging in these other dishonest activities with him. "Yes, I'm thinking about this stuff again buddy" Alex said. Joseph wasn't confessing his other sins to him. they were the cause of the decaying of our western civilization. They were implementing their own brand of justice again folks. Alex has found this lawyer to represent him. If they were debating each other again folks. If they weren't going to be voting for this candidate. They weren't having a fair election cycle this year. If they were using these other nefarious tactics against them. So they aren't capable of rigging the outcome of this upcoming election again folks. If they are selecting this lady. So Hillary can become the next president of the United States of America. Hillary is enacting with them. Because she is talking to these people about her different policies again folks. Hillary is thinking this stuff would have been beneficial for her candidacy. Hillary is going to be altering the fate of this country. Hillary's policies would have a substantial impact on this nation's financial system. Hillary is aiming to reduce these other amounts of people. They have been committing these crimes against us. They were accusing this lady of being another awful person. Alex hasn't been able to come up with his own strategy for himself. Our citizen's sovereignty is at stake here again folks. Joseph is confident in his own ability again folks. Joseph doesn't care about anyone

else lives again folks. "You aren't capable of convincing me. they are these bunch of other scumbags. If you would have allowed someone else to debate these other people on certain topic again buddy" Joseph said.  " I'm not capable of debating you. Especially If you aren't being truthful with me" Alex said. Joseph has his own sexual fantasies about them. Chelsea would have rejected him. Joseph was pursuing them. However, Joseph has this distorted perception of his own reality again gentlemen. Joseph has been failing to comprehend this stuff himself. Alex wasn't going to be pleading his case to them. Joseph believes these other women would've been susceptible to his sexual advances nowadays gentlemen. Joseph doesn't want anyone else to view him. As a sexual predator. Joseph doesn't believe that he can become a serious threat to them. They aren't responding to him. They were using these other methods on them. They were convincing these significant number of women. They wouldn't want to touch their partner own penis again gentlemen. Unless they're bribing them. Joseph has been discussing the civil rights movement with his friends. Joseph believes that everyone else has a right to vote for their favorite candidate. Joseph believes that the civil rights movement has played a significant role in the reshaping of this country legal systems gentlemen. Joseph has been emphasizing this stuff to them. Joseph believes that these women doesn't find any fulfillment in being just an average housewife. they would have been allowing any of those doctors to do these medical procedures on them. They aren't capable of debating this other issue with them. our country issues are stemming from many of these issues again folks. These politicians are dividing these other citizens. Joseph is becoming a candidate. Joseph isn't capable of addressing these other women's emotional issues again folks. Joseph has been wanting to have these other sexual encounters with them. " I have gotten a better solution for them. If they aren't expecting someone else to fix these other people's problem for them. They should have been doing their own research into this specific topic again buddy. If they weren't allowing any of these other women to be dating any of their male counterpart again buddy. If this young lady would've provided you and me with another quick response again buddy. I'm wondering if Hillary would've accepted your friend offer again buddy. If they're letting their other male's friend to sample a small percentage of this young lady's pussy again buddy. this lady would've slapped the hell out of them. You're not receiving another golden ticket from them. So you're not shining like a star anymore buddy. you're not seducing anyone's else spouse again buddy. But if you can show them. You can respect them. Chelsea wouldn't have given her associates access to her friend pussy again buddy. Especially if they're wearing a mega hat and outfit again buddy. Whenever you're out in this public square. If you're pretending that you're a little creepy again buddy? They're not letting their own wives to be giving away their pussy to someone else again buddy. I'm very handsome again buddy. What if they're noticing that my friend is wearing this hat upon his own head. What If they were reading the hat logo again buddy. What If they noticed that this shit has been imprinted on top of this hat. I'm making America great again buddy? You must've realized that we're not getting laid because of them. If you're continuing to follow through with these charades on them. You're not going through with it again buddy", Joseph said. "I'm not wearing such an offensive outfit because of them. If you're noticing that we have this trend in our country and I'm thinking that we're letting this trend divide us. They're making this stuff transparent to them. We have allowed these two political parties cause this friction between these two opposites genders again buddy. I'm thinking that many of us. We have made this stuff acceptable to every one of us. We have been mistreating these women for a while now buddy. I'm going to be facing another horrific dilemma myself. I'm going to be able to bet with you. You're witnessing many of those others strange occurrence in this time period again buddy. If they're wanting to allow these other people to diminish someone else light again buddy. If they're not allowing anyone else to accomplish some of their own goals again buddy. I'm thinking this shit is costing me. I'm working really hard on bringing my very significant goal to fruition in the future. Maybe they're losing respect for them. I'm thinking this shit is affecting these other people relationships again buddy. Maybe you're not getting into any other major conflict with them. Even if you don't realize that you do have this huge potential inside of you. You're getting in over your own head again buddy. You don't understand that there are certain people. who does find this sort of bullshit very offensive to them. this person's hat might've represented something different to them. They have framed their own narrative around their idea again buddy. They believed that a certain group of people. They can't afford to send their own children to these other private university. I'm not a racist bastard again buddy. they would've gone nuts over this other shit again buddy. I'm not brave again buddy? Because they would've assaulted me. They can kiss the crack of my friend's asshole again buddy. Especially if I'm wearing this particular hat. Buddy on a specific evening. I'm going to be betting with you. I'm not capable of starting a huge riot amongst these massive groups of people. They would've asked me. If I'm going to be removing this stupid hat from my own head again buddy. I'm going to be beating someone else ass again buddy. They're not living amongst us. You're not some random person. They would've beaten the holy shit out of you. I'm going to try to warn you" Alex said. "You aren't fooling me. You're not pulling anyone's else leg again buddy. If you're going to be touching this person daughter inappropriately again buddy. I'm not watching this bloody grudge match to take place between them. You are a dead man again buddy. They would have wanted someone else to shoved their feet inside of my friend's asshole for them. This person would've blamed you. What If this person told them? You were the person. Who was responsible for creating this havoc amongst them? I'm not letting anyone else hurt them. I'm not allowing anyone else to sexually assault them?" Alex said. "I'm doing my own research myself. you aren't making any of these other women cry over you. I'm not going to be letting some doctor to be performing surgery on this lady's face again buddy. Because Hillary's face is disgusting looking to me. I can't stand them. I'm not injuring someone else. Hillary should have been covering up her daughter's hideous face again buddy. So just in case, you have missed it again buddy. I'm educating you. Especially if I don't want to be sleeping with them. If someone else is wanting to kiss me" Joseph said. "Whenever you are insulting them. You're not a very good fighter. You must've been able to remember this shit happening to us. You're not Ronda Rosenthal. If you're searching through this person's background right now again buddy. Ronda has these amazing fighting credentials again buddy. Ronda is known as the baddest woman" Alex said. "Because I'm an alien. I'm not sure if there is anyone else. who is like me? Nobody else is better than me? I would have been poking the bear. I'm using my other five fingers on them. I'm making this person's eyes ball swell up on them. There is this person. whose name is Sliver Tongue Mike. Mike has done some horrible things to those other boxing competitors. Whenever Mike was facing his other adversaries inside of a boxing ring. You're exactly like them. they are getting in a terrible vehicle accident. I'm not injuring you. You're eating your other meals through a tiny straw again buddy. I'm destroying them" Joseph said. " You aren't capable of defending yourself. Because you are a little munchkin. You are sadly mistaking about it again buddy. you aren't capable of proving this shit to me. you're doing these others awful things to them. I'm going to be patiently waiting for you. So you're making the first move towards me. Whenever we're in a public setting together. If you aren't confronting them. You want to fight me. I'm not a very good street fighter. So this person is standing out there on the street corner? If they aren't minding their own business. they aren't bothering anyone else on this planet. If someone else is going to be sucker-punching them. But if they don't knock your friend unconscious again buddy. If they aren't kicking your rear end for me. Are if they aren't feeding your friend a knuckle sandwich again buddy" Alex said. "You aren't making any sort of sense to me. You aren't capable of defeating me. You shouldn't have been lying to me" Alex said. "I had enough of you. You can give this shit a rest again buddy" Joseph said.

*They showed those three documents to this woman fellows. (5 years)*

Vinny kept racing towards their direction. Vinny was receiving some interesting news from someone else. Vinny was having a discussion about them. Someone else should have informed him. Vinny wasn't capable of getting someone's else attention again folks. Alex might have been able to use this information to his advantage again fellas. Vinny had to get another person's authorization for these two people to be proceeding with interviewing their client. Vinny was bringing up these two fugitive's names to his employer. Nobody else has been trying to help them. Alex is facing another time constraint again folks. Vinny was making this stuff clear to these two fugitives. Vinny is going to be wrapping up all his other work-related tasks today. They weren't interested in prolonging their interview with her again folks. Hillary was preparing for her upcoming speech to these other voters. Vinny has issued a warning to everyone else. Vinny has stated this stuff to these other employees. If Hillary doesn't agree to become a participant in these two reporter's interviews of her again fellas. Vinny is going to force these two people to depart from the stadium. Hillary has been an important part of reshaping everyone else minds. Hillary isn't capable of spending time with these two people. They weren't hesitant about asking this client another question about her policy. Hillary isn't interested in doing some of her other jobs related duties again folks. They were being given a limited amount of access to this client. Hillary isn't in another relaxing frame of mind. Nobody else would have been allowed to be in the presence of this client. They shouldn't have been disrespectful of anyone else again folks. Hillary is going to be enhancing her other campaign strategies for this country upcoming election cycle again folks. Hillary is going to be approaching some of these other milestones in her political career again folks. Hillary is going to be encouraging these other voters to be voting for herself. Hillary is going to conveying many of her other message to them. Hillary's manager has been analyzing her bosses past campaigns strategies again folks. This person is going to be conducting her own research into theses other various topics again folks. Hillary is going to be seeking these other expert's input into some of these other things again folks. Hillary is creating her other all-encompassing plan for her supporters. Hillary is going to be continuing to follow through with this ongoing progression of her campaign again folks. Hillary wasn't effective for reshaping this country political landscape. Nobody else would be contributing anything of them to this woman successful administration. The lady has been underneath these other two guys observation for a while now again folks. They are going to be monitoring this lady other current routine again folks. Because Joseph is going to be executing his plans for himself. Joseph doesn't want another person to be arousing this lady suspicion of them. They have been able to carry out this mission themselves. Alex wasn't going to be doing this stuff to these other people. Nobody else should have been allowed to be helping this woman to complete many of her other assignment again folks. if they weren't capable of establishing an alliance with these other people. Vinny is wanting this person to upholds her agreement with them. they have this mutually agreed upon agreement between themselves. Vinny wasn't able to take any sort of action against these two people. if Vinny is going to be modifying these agreed-upon terms again folks. Vinny isn't sure if this stuff is going to be necessary for him. Because if these people aren't capable of achieving their own desired results again folks. Vinny is seeking confirmation from these two gentlemen. if they were capable of sharing their employment status with their company. Vinny is becoming very curious about these two gentlemen other long-term goals for themselves. They weren't interested in enhancing their own likeability amongst these other politicians. If Hillary doesn't continue to follow through with this stuff of her again fellas. Hillary doesn't have to answer to anyone else. Vinny is going to be confirming this shit for himself. Vinny has been able to try to read an few of these excerpts from their company's handbook again folks. if folks this company handbook doesn't clearly states this stuff within itself nowadays. What Vinny must do to try to reprimand these other employees of the company. If they weren't being professional again folks. Vinny will be trying to suggest this other stuff to theses other employees. These other employees will have to try to resigned from their current company position again folks. If they aren't willing to be abiding by their own bosses' policies again folks. Everyone else should have been studying an initial section of their employee's handbook again folks. the owner would have included these other specific phrases in their company's handbook again folks. If these people have written a certain clause in their company's handbook again folks. If they are going to be misrepresenting their company's business model again folks. If they were engaging in any of these other illegal activities with someone else. They will have to terminated these employees. "Hey, I'm not changing a lot of these other company's policy around here again buddy. If Hillary would have indicated this stuff to me? If you weren't interested in bothering this person. I'm not forcing anyone else to be leaving this company. I'm not allowing another person to be interfering with our other employees' duties today. If another person isn't capable of fulfilling some of their other promises to this company executive. I'm going to be making these other decisions for the executives again fellas" Vinny said. "This person is trying to locate our clients. I'm not sure if this person is capable of guiding another human being. So I'm going over these processes with these other employees" Vinny said this stuff to them. "If you weren't providing my partner with directions to this lady's dressing room. I'm becoming very appreciative of these other people" Joseph said. "if you're going to be accompanying another person. Because if you're wasting my precious time again buddy. I'm going to declining your friend's request for everyone else" Vinny said. Vinny was going to be taking these two guys into this client's dressing room. Whenever Vinny was knocking upon this dressing room door? Hillary wasn't responding to anyone else. Vinny was going to be calling out to this person. Vinny haven't heard any sort of peep from this client. "I'm wanting your friends to come on in here's again fellows" Hillary said. Whenever they were walking into the room. they were going to be looking straight into this woman's face again folks. Hillary was acting very strangely towards these two people. They were feeling a little bewilderment by this lady antics again folks. They were going to be looking into every square inch of this small compartment. They were searching for any of those other sign of another surveillance devices again folks. They aren't sure if someone else is capable of installing these surveillance cameras inside of the room. they weren't able to locate those other six small recordings devices again folks. "I'm waiting to ask your friends something else about you. I'm not sure if you're allowing my partner to be sitting down upon your soft couch" Alex said. "Yes, please you can take any of those other seat again fellas. You shouldn't have allowed another person to be bothering me" Hillary said. "I'm not sure if you're capable of obtaining some of these other important documentations again buddy. I would have been able to share this documentation with these other employees. If you could take another quick peek again sweetheart. I'm going to be bringing these other documents with me" Joseph's said. "Yes, I'm allowing you, and your friend to share this information with me. But you're not a reporter. So if you're not capable of doing this exclusive interview with me" Hillary said. "You could have done this shit for them. If I'm giving anyone else the wrong impression of me. I'm here because of this specific reason again sweetheart. Because I'm going to be blackmailing you. I'm not giving anyone else any sort of an advantage over me. I'm conjuring up this lame excuse myself. Because I'm not forcing anyone else. They didn't have to let me and my partner to come in here again sweetheart. I'm going to be speaking with you. I'm needing you and your friend to give me and my friend your corporation in this matter again sweetheart. I don't know when anyone else is at their most vulnerable again sweetheart. I'm not capable of coming up with these other ideas myself. I'm not capable of getting myself and my friend inside of this entranceway again sweetheart. I'm making these copies of those other important documentation again sweetheart. I'm not letting anyone else to destroy me. I'm not letting anyone else to know about anything else again darling. before I'm done with speaking with you. Before I'm getting another chance to show you. I'm not sure if you're capable of understanding how valuable this information is to us. I'm not sure if anyone else should be sharing this other important information with them. I'm not sure if I'm capable of getting my hands on this other incriminating evidence against you. If someone else would have looked through these pages of those other documents again sweetheart. This person would have found some interesting details about you. If someone else is going to be able to trace this stuff back to you. I'm telling everyone else about your husband other criminals' offense again sweetheart. I'm going to be leading these two policemen back to your family doorstep again sweetheart. I couldn't have allowed them and you to hide your other criminal offenses from them. I'm not sure if I'm capable of transferring most of this information over onto another floppy disc again sweetheart. I'm not sure if anyone else is capable of hiding those other extras copies of these documents from them. I'm going to be hiding these documents amongst these other items in my house. I wouldn't have allowed myself and my friend to keep these other floppy discs lying around my house. You're sadly mistaken about me" Alex said. "If anyone else is wondering, what sort of stuff that I'm hiding inside of some of these other documents again sweetheart? I'm not capable of pulling another sick prank on anyone else again sweetheart," Joseph has declared again folks. " I'm not sure if you're capable of making up another amusing story. you may have been wondering about me and my friend other intentions towards you. I have in my possession these other documents again sweetheart. Thus, I'm not letting you or anyone else to do anything foolish to me. If you're not capable of maintaining your own composure during this terribly painful procedure again sweetheart. I'm giving you and everyone else another chance to read through this material again sweetheart," Alex remarked. "I'm going to be corresponding directly with you and your security team again sweetheart. If you're not capable of clarifying this stuff for me. I'm not sure if you're capable of harming me? I'm going to be helping them. so they can arrest them. because If you're capable of breaking this law again buddy. I'm not sure if you're capable of targeting any member of the Congress". Hillary declared. "I'm not letting anyone else to be using this stuff against me." Alex said. "If Hillary isn't capable of making an effort again buddy. She doesn't want to listen to us. Whenever I'm providing these people with information about how they can help this lady to get out of this sticky situation again buddy. I'm giving everyone else the opportunity to acquire these vital documents for themselves. I'm not sure if this kind of thing could hurt your boss career again buddy. I'm not going to be giving you and your friend any other chance of saving yourself. Because if you're wanting someone else to help you and your friend to become apart of this branch of our government. Thus, I will personally give this woman the option to choose from these two additional choices. Are all of the cards in this deck in our hands? This woman needs to decide, dude. I am demanding it. if you are not engaging in cooperative play. Must I ruin my own career to make this woman happy? That being said, if you disregard any of my other instructions. I may have to carry out my initial plans. I will attempt to release those documents to the public as well. This is the last chance I am going to give this woman. so that you can attempt to decide this last choice on your own. This woman must give it to me. Joseph provided a response on her own. I will not play around with you. stated Alex. I would be able to resolve this issue on my own. You really do possess these two enormous balls. You are threatening me then. Hillary declared, "I am not going to let these two guys get away with this shit." "We will require this woman's assistance for ourselves. Joseph stated, "Because we intend to take over the government agencies ourselves." "If I succeeded in helping these two guys reach this absurd objective of mine. Guys, what have I got for myself? If I accept this dreadful arrangement for myself," Hillary remarked. "You receive nothing additional for yourself. You actually escape with nothing at all. Thus, if I could articulate it clearly. Just in case you are not too smart yourself. We should not be arrested; they should not try. since we did not ourselves commit treason. if you are unwilling to assist us. if we are unable to accomplish these other objectives. We desired to overthrow this pitiful administration on our own. Should you decline our offer of assistance. After that, we personally deliver those documents to these additional law enforcement organizations. I plan to personally deliver a few of these documents to the other media outlets. I will personally provide this information to every reporter. The majority of the other horrifying crimes will be known to everyone else directly. You are the one who hask committed these additional crimes against the people. if you yourself are still in contact with these individuals. Declared Joseph. "You really think that now, my dear, the ball is in your court? What action will you take on your own, then? Alex stated. If I were allowed to. I am attempting to entertain this idea in my mind. Before I attempted to give these two guys my most sincere response. Hillary stated, "After that, I would give these two guys my decision." We do not have several hours to ourselves. Yes, we do require your decision. We will not be forced by you. Put yourself in a bind, lady. If I am required to submit this content to these media outlets by myself? Personally, I do think that time is of the essence. Alex stated, "I do not have time to play these other mind games with you." Alright, I consent to follow the conditions of our mutual agreement. Now pardon me if these two guys could. I have to prepare myself. I have to speak in front of a group of people myself. Do yourself a favor and help these two guys? Perhaps you could take these two guys out of my dressing room? If they were able to drop those documents off there by themselves? mainly because I want to personally review these significant documents. Hillary remarked, "I have to verify the authenticity of the document myself. Okay, but you really should not try to mess with us. We succeeded in convincing another person. In order for him to create a duplicate copy of these additional documentsuments for me. In the event that you attempt to con me. You might end up jeopardizing your own career," Joseph stated.

## Alex asked this agent at the door for a cigarette fellow. (5 years)

Alex is unsure of why he has let the situation escalate between them, considering he has always been the rational once again folks. Alex finds himself, once again folks being taken advantage of by certain individuals in his life. I think despite this guy's past experiences, where people have deliberately sabotaged his relationships with others, Alex is unsure why he has allowed this pattern to continue throughout his life. Two agents were observed standing near the door, indicating their presence and continued work at the location. They are having an conservation with themselves. Joseph has been eager for his friend, Alex, to once again ask this individual for a cigarette. However, Alex has been reluctant to approach this agent due to uncertainty regarding the agent's potential response. Alex approached his friend to seek suggestions from him. He was considering approaching an agent, but he had concerns about the potential for a negative outcome again folks. Specifically, Alex was worried that the agent might use profanity towards him. Alex was feeling embarrassed about the possibility of being reprimanded by the agent in front of everyone. He realized he needed to reconsider his approach and figure out how to handle the situation better. "Ok, What if this gentleman declines to hand it over to me?" Alex said. They plan to sneak past the security guards in order to gain entry into the building. It is crucial for them to stay vigilant and aware of their surroundings, as any of the guards could potentially apprehend them. Because we're acting a slight suspiciously ourselves. In this situation, there are two options available. The first option is to proceed with the plan once more. The second option is to abandon the idea altogether. However, Alex believes that the little green creature will not back down. This is because Joseph has a significant ego and believes that the world revolves around him. Joseph is the type of alien who would enter a burning building without attempting to rescue any of the occupants, unless they offered something valuable to him. To illustrate the creature's selfishness, let's consider a hypothetical scenario. If there was a woman whom Joseph found attractive, he would only save her if she allowed the creature to invade her uterus with his fingers and face. If you can't deal with accomplishing limited tasks yourself. You don't wish to go through with this idea of your chum's. Joseph is concerned that his friend might jeopardize their plans, as he has put a lot of effort into them. It is important for them to have a thorough discussion before proceeding, to avoid making any mistakes that could have serious consequences. Alex shares this belief, recognizing the potential costs of such errors. If you wished that someone's else would continue to accompany you. Whenever you proceed on this lengthy trip yourself. You shouldn't hope that someone's else would hold your palms along the way their chum. If you haven't seen these separate two security guards setting there again, chum. Do you notice how many of these individuals have equipped themselves. Joseph with a revolver chum. If you can try to count on your fingers, how many of these security guards are there again buddy. If you didn't spot that they have fixed these surveillance cameras around this construction. So they can see a glimpse of any trespassers. Who is seeking to burst into this institution again buddy" Joseph said. "Ok, if you didn't prefer that I was successful in my attempt to gain access to this building" Alex said. Alex raced towards the primary entrance of this construction. Alex was seeking to strike up a discussion with them. "If you could indulge me. I wished to know, if you would do me a favor again chum. I wanted a smoke from you" Alex said. "I'm not a store clerk. You shouldn't expect me. Buddy to raise you. You must seek to solicit recruitment with any of these other businesses chum. Who is bringing in individuals?" this guy said. "Well, I want to try to thank you. Because you're going to take time to address some of these other concerns of mine" Alex said. Then Alex started walking away from this person himself. Alex did overhear this guy speaking with another person about this shit himself. Who was this dumbass buddy? I'm getting sick of all of these other bums myself. Whenever someone does try to approach me," this guy said. Alex asked a friend of his fellows. If he should've try to reiterate against this guy himself. why this guy didn't want to loan this guy a cigarette himself. They need to find themselves folks, a steady job buddy. "They should stop trying to mooch off of these other people. Who is in this society nowadays. what is wrong with these other people in this world of ours today? I do believe there are too many of these other assholes myself. Who is exactly like this one particular person buddy? If they're going to try to sit on the couch doing nothing at home buddy? If they believe someone else should support their habits themselves. If they think that we owe these people something else ourselves" this guy said. Alex repeated everything this man had to say about him. Alex pointed one of these fingers of his toward this person himself. "You notice that whenever I did try to approach this person myself. You didn't notice this guy acted rudely toward me. I do believe this person is a smartass myself. When I did try to ask this man. If he was going to try to loan me. Buddy one of these guys cigarettes today. If this person took this shit personally himself" Alex said.

prison

*Joseph saw a strange aircraft hovering near him. (5 years)*

They've journeyed to a sanctuary. Alex was finding solace in this place. Alex was becoming aware of these other extraordinary events. There was this large aircraft floating across the sky. Alex wasn't able to notice this huge flying object hovering around him. Joseph was trying to mock this young man. Alex has been unable to reach these other items on this shelf. Alex is gazing in the wrong direction. "If you aren't looking into any sort of particular area of the sky," Joseph said. Joseph is sharing this incredible experience with this young man. Joseph didn't manufacture this aircraft. Alex was thinking about this small beam of light radiating from the bottom of this aircraft. Alex wasn't trying to acknowledge the existence of these large objects to anyone else. Someone else has been able to attach this firing mechanism to the wing of this large aircraft. Joseph has been waiting to try to change the subject of their conversation to these other foreign dictators. This dictator has been ordering his troops to try to attack another densely populated area of their country. This leader doesn't want his other soldiers to take any more of these other hostages to their camp. This leader's objective is to eliminate every single hostage. If these people are obstructing these dictator troops from completing their missions again, folks? This leader's goal is to try to seize control of another foreign country's other natural resources again folks. This dictator wants to try to assert his power over everyone else. If anyone else isn't allowing this dictator to try to escalate these other things between these two countries. This dictator doesn't care if these other soldiers try to destabilize another entire region of another country. These soldiers must try to follow their leader's orders to attack their other enemies throughout another populated area of any of these other countries. These soldiers would have faced other severe consequences for disobeying their commander's direct order to try to eliminate every single person. They believe it poses any sort of other threat to their country's sovereignty. This commander displays any sort of disregard for his troop's safety again folks. "You aren't letting your imagination get the upper hand on you," Alex said. Joseph isn't very supportive of this young man's thoughts and ideas, about how he believes that this dictator shouldn't have been trying to silence these other groups of people. This aircraft had been able to land close to another tree. Alex hasn't been able to accept this truth about himself. I'm sure that some of these other large trees are obstructing everyone's else view of this large aircraft hovering above them. Joseph has been desiring to try to prolong his vacation. Joseph will be arriving in another matter of hours. Joseph has been able to try to deplete another person cognitive capacity with the stroke of his hands again, folks. Joseph isn't interested in seeking this sort of guidance from any of these other therapists. Joseph has been developing his own irrational spiritual beliefs. "Whenever I'm arriving in the state of Virginia," Alex said. "I mustn't try to do this shit to anyone else," Joseph said. Joseph was very perplexed by some of these other various optical illusions of his again fellas. I'm not sure if this creature has been preparing to witness these other visual phenomenal events. Joseph couldn't alter another person's perception about certain things that these other people think is happening in their reality. Alex don't know what is happening to this creature on these other rare occasions. Alex was being consumed with these other concern for the well-being of his pet. "If you aren't able to return home," Joseph said. Joseph isn't a very intelligent creature. Joseph has been able to make his idol threats against this young man. Alex was trying to reminded everyone else of this creature other comments about himself. I'm sure that this shit is going to be catching up to this creature. "You are a real basket case my friend" Alex said.

## *Joseph Flanagan was trying to cast a magic spell on the dog ladies and gentlemen. (5 years)*

Joseph has shown on this guy's doorstep last night. Alex wouldn't have invited him. Joseph was following him. Joseph was flopping his ass down onto this person's sofa. Joseph was making other ridiculous claims himself. Joseph doesn't approve of this particular guy's lifestyle. Unfortunately, Joseph was unable to complete it again folks. Because someone has interrupted their argument again folks. "You haven't even considered it again buddy," Alex said. Alex has attempted to repay him. Because Alex owes him. If they aren't successful with their blackmailing attempt again folks. they would've been receiving their rewards directly again folks. Joseph strongly dislikes them. Alex is insulting him. Alex believes it is unhelpful to their relationship nowadays. Alex is letting his personal bias against him. Joseph thinks that it is going to interfere with their friendship again folks. Alex isn't going to accept his friend's proposal again folks. He is concerned about engaging in other illegal activities with him. Folks it could harm this guy reputation among his other peers. Alex recognizes his actions can have a long-lasting consequences in his life again folks. Alex doesn't want to cause any further damage to himself. "What you're talking about at this moment again buddy?" Alex said. Alex consistently refers to him. as a creepy little green person. Joseph is going to hinder his pursuit to find happiness again folks. Joseph can affect these other people's well-being again folks. "I'm feeling very sick to my stomach again buddy. Whenever I'm constantly dealing with him. Whenever you're getting in touch with me" Joseph said. Joseph was yelling at him. Joseph was referring to this guy dog as a shit head again folks. Joseph is persistently trying to capture his friend dog's attention for an extended period again folks. Joseph intends to harm this dog. "I'm offering your dog a very tasty treat again buddy," Joseph said. "Trinity has always been my favorite animal. However, someone else gave me. Trinity for my fifteenth birthday present again buddy" Alex said. Since then, Alex has been feeding the dog constantly again folks. Alex has been taking the dog on an adventure through the forest. Trinity has run in a different direction again folks. Trinity was wagging her very long tail again folks. Trinity had been acting strangely toward him. Trinity has been avoiding him. she hasn't gone near the creature since last weekend. what did Joseph do to this guy dog again folks. Trinity is growling at him. If Trinity doesn't bite him. Joseph has been performing these other magical spells on this guy's dog. Joseph has cursed this guy's dog again folks. Joseph is practicing witchcraft nowadays. "I'm not going to tell you. If you don't obey me. Whenever you're not following any of my other instructions again buddy. I'm wanting someone else to accompany me. I'm needing your help again buddy. I'm working on this project again buddy. Whenever I'm arranging it again buddy. So whenever I'm able to take control of this agency. Because I have a limited amount of time again buddy. If I'm not able to accomplish this shit myself. I'm needing you. Alex to provide me. Buddy with your answer by the weekend again buddy" Joseph said. Joseph has dedicated a significant amount of time to developing this project again folks. Joseph has been refining his strategy for a while now. Joseph has been analyzing every detail in his mind again folks. "If you haven't thought of another plan yet again buddy. No, I haven't had a chance to accomplish these other tasks of mine," Alex said. "I don't want any more of your other stupid excuses again buddy. You don't have the brain capabilities in my opinion again buddy? I'm holding all of the cards again buddy. if you're not wanting to follow these other instructions of mine. You don't have any other choice again buddy. I'm not choosing from these other options again buddy. I'm reconsidering my first objective again today. John my objective should've been going with my first option again buddy. I'm not harming your relatives again buddy. I might've wanted to harm your dog again buddy" Joseph said. "Hey, you're crossing the line again chum. You're going to be leaving this residence again chum. If you're trying to threaten me" Alex said. " Now you've got this dog upset again chum. I'm not putting up with it anymore again buddy. I'm wanting to ask you. If Alex would've put a collar around the dog neck again buddy. I don't like this animal" Joseph said. "Before you came to visit me. Joseph everything isn't great between us" Joseph said. " I'm refusing to obey you. You're making my life much harder on me. I'm refusing to finish completing your mission again buddy" Alex said. Joseph was snapping his finger in this person's dog's direction again folks. " Alex your dog must try to obey my rules again buddy. You've been a good girl. You shouldn't protect your owner. I'm giving this dog permission to attack it owner" Joseph said. Joseph ex-friend had heard enough of this shit again folks. Alex isn't tough again folks. Alex told him. Joseph must leave the guy household. Alex didn't remind him. Alex will be returning soon again folks.

### *Alex is on an aircraft. They are flying back home themselves. (5 years)*

The aircraft is currently in-flight folks. they're on their way to their destination. Joseph was going through a difficult period again folks. They needed to reassure him. Joseph has these question lingering in his mind. Joseph is currently searching for a suitable location. Joseph has been wanting to meet them. Hillary hasn't rescheduled the press conference in the future. Hillary is focusing on her other commitments again folks. Hillary has another daily routine. If they're getting in contact with them. Hillary was preparing for her conference again folks. Hillary has laid down the groundwork again folks. Hillary was ensured everyone else this stuff would go accordingly to her plan again folks. They've been focusing on preventing any major catastrophes from occurring during this critical period again folks. They're determined to protect themselves. they've been putting forth an effort themselves. They're gathering this incriminating evidence against them. What If these two gentlemen's plans went awry again folks. They're having these doubts again folks. they're predicting their blackmailing plot will be successful again folks. they're proceeding with it again folks. they could've been in conflict with them. They're currently experiencing this significant number of challenges again folks. why they're allowing this stuff to impact them. Especially if they're attempting to blackmail them. They have picked a specific person to target again folks. They're effectively pursuing them. They're developing an alternative plan again folks. Hillary has been exerted her significant influence over them. They're working within the current administration again folks. They're currently a member of the house of repentance again folks. They're diligently working within these other various government agencies. Hillary was working within the current administration again folks. "I don't have any negative opinions of them. I have these preconceived notions of them. Hillary is an evil witch. we must prevent this woman from single-handedly shattering our aspirations again buddy" Joseph said. "You don't need to get worked up over this stuff again buddy. Joseph these things are very small inconveniences to me. I'm not taking any action against them. I'm determined to regain control over my own life again buddy. I'm needing to address some of this stuff myself. Especially if I'm going to try to renegotiate the terms of our agreement with them. I'm not allowing someone else to underestimate me. I'm not stupid again buddy. I'm not an expert again buddy. I'm achieving my other objectives again buddy. I'm willing to do everything again buddy" Alex said. "I'm determined to blackmail our initial target again buddy. They shouldn't intervene on this lady's behalf again buddy. Whenever I'm pursuing this quest of mine. I'm discussing it with you. I'm getting this job done properly again buddy. If I'm needing my friend assistance with this matter again buddy. I'm asking you. If you're wanting to help me. I'm not letting someone else to make a fool out of me. I do know this shit for a fact again buddy. If you're dishonest with me. If you didn't attend any other previous University" Joseph said. "You're a smart-ass right now buddy. I'm not getting mad at you. I'm not taking my frustration out on you" Alex said. "If you're doing this shit to me. I'm not allowing anything terrible happen to me. You're not threatening my pet's life again buddy. You're sadly mistaken again buddy. I'm not doing someone else wrong again buddy. I'm not allowing anyone else to injure me" Alex said. "Because if you're not afraid of me. I'm accomplishing this simple task of mine" Joseph said. "I'm an very tolerating person. If you're planning to eliminate me. If you're wanting to try to achieve your goal again buddy. I'm not complying with you. If you're harming my relatives again buddy? If you're sabotaging me. Joseph this mission isn't prospering in the future. If you're refusing to follow these instructions of mine. I'm going to be bashing your skull in again buddy. Before you get the opportunity to defend yourself" Alex said. " Why you're threatening me? I'm not condoning your behavior again buddy. If you're wanting to remain a part of my pet life again buddy. You're not betraying me. I'm stopping it again buddy. I'm sending your ass flying out of this window again buddy. I'm destroying you" Alex said.

## *Alex discussed this situation with his friend himself. (5 years)*

Alex has been packing his suitcases. Alex was heading towards the airport. Alex has been regretting making these decisions for himself. Alex wasn't able to complete with them. Alex was buying two of those plane tickets for them. They are traveling on this trip together. Alex wasn't expecting anything else happening to them. Whenever they were abroad of this aircraft. "So we're traveling to the province of Russia" Alex said. They were going to be leaving this specific area. Alex is walking alongside his friend. They were on the shoreline together. Alex isn't communicating with his friend. Alex wasn't able to speak any of these people's language again folks. Joseph was posing this question to his friend. Joseph doesn't know what time him and his friend were arriving in the country of Russia. They were showing hostility towards them. they were encountering these other challenging moments in their own lives again folks. whenever they are returning home. They were gone on this long hiatus again folks. They were facing other consequences for their own actions against them. Alex isn't capable of being fearful of them. They were trying to separate them. Alex has this other apprehension about themselves. this dictator is going in exile again folks. Damien likes someone else to harm these two fugitives. Damien is such an notorious individual. He is a very violent person. They aren't capable of challenging this person's leadership skills again folks. Alex is arriving there alone again folks. Joseph has this unusual task ahead of himself. Joseph doesn't have any more of this willpower leftovers within himself. Joseph isn't capable of achieving these other goals in his life. If they aren't settling this disagreement amongst themselves. Joseph is obtaining these other items for himself. Alex is making his friend these other promises again folks. Alex doesn't have any of those other passageways. Alex doesn't want anyone else to agree with him. They are using their own tactic against them. " I wasn't expecting this crap from you. I shouldn't have been trying to help them" Alex said. Alex is allowing these people to transport them back to the United States of America. They weren't capable of facing this other uncertainty on an daily basis again folks. They aren't remaining free again folks. If they were capable of sending two of those fugitives back to their own homeland. Hillary wouldn't have gone through with her own press conference again folks. Alex strongly dislikes many of those other people. Alex isn't lingering in this particular location any longer again folks. Joseph has been working alongside many of those other people again folks. Because Joseph is getting someone else to help them. Joseph isn't capable of implementing many of these plans himself. They weren't staying here for any duration again folks. Joseph has been using these other various strategies against them. Joseph isn't capable of putting in place his other safety measures again folks. Joseph isn't capable of expressing himself. They don't have any of those similar beliefs themselves. Alex was wanting to learn about these other people's culture. Why doesn't Joseph share his friend's perspective again folks. Even if they aren't capable of sharing similar viewpoint again folks. They were capable of influencing them. Joseph is seeking them. Alex isn't an openminded person. Alex wasn't capable of grasping other people's political concepts again folks. Whenever they were together. They were preparing themselves. So they can finish this assignment together. They aren't realizing there are these other events that are unfolding again folks. If Joseph wasn't capable of pursuing his own dreams in the near future. "I'm asking you. If someone else has been saying anything else about me. I don't agree with these people on many of those other key issues again buddy. I'm not capable of enlisting many of these other people help again buddy. I'm waiting for someone else to authenticate this other data for me. Before I'm getting into contact with them. I'm digging through the veracity of this important data myself. I'm not confiding in any of them. I'm feeling a little stressed out about it myself. Because I'm realizing this crap has become challenging for me. I'm not capable of rewriting this person's foreign policy for them. I'm different from many of those people again buddy. They don't have an good re-pore with me. There are several regions. I'm putting these other different regions in the same catalogue as this country of Indonesia. They are running out of other resources at some point again buddy. So they can't force someone's else to transport us. I don't like to negotiating with anyone else again buddy. Because they aren't receiving their freedom again buddy. I'm thinking about this stuff again buddy. I'm not sure if this stuff would have been in their leader's best interested again buddy. Nobody else should've have been releasing them. So if they are going to be able to convince anyone else of their innocence again buddy. I'm not allowing anyone else to hand me and you over to them. They aren't thinking about these other people revolting against them. because they were facing these other poor conditions within their own country. They weren't capable of overthrowing their country current regimes. Because they aren't thinking about it themselves. If they're allowing this other people to do this shit to them. If they aren't applying for this dual citizenship overseas again folk. They aren't capable of undergoing this lengthy process themselves. If they aren't remaining in this other foreign country. They weren't able to tolerate many of those people. they aren't capable of living amongst them. "they aren't being treated fairly by these other people again buddy. they are sending these other people to to apprehend us. We are facing this significant impact in our own lives again buddy? If they aren't capable of coaxing us. They weren't expecting that there would be these other people. Who would like to do these other people bidding for them. these people aren't capable of adhering to these other laws again buddy. What if they aren't willing to urge these other people on again buddy. You don't know if we're being sought after again buddy. They are wanting someone else to come searching for us. But we weren't the people. Who has committed these acts of treason against our own government" Joseph said. " No, they wouldn't have been able to haul us back there again buddy. We don't any sort of connection with this terrorist organization again buddy. They can't find anyone else. who is going to be supportive of them. So they don't have the authority to release them. they weren't capable of carrying out their leader goals for him. If they weren't capable of developing their own method again buddy. So they weren't capable of impermanent Ing this stuff themselves. If they were capable of doing these other horrible things to them. If they were capable of inflicting some of this pain upon them. Notably, if they were capable of charging these other people with violating many of their other laws again buddy. They wouldn't have been capable of doing this other crap to us. I don't think this is mutiny again buddy. They would have killed many of those other people" Alex said. "They weren't capable of solving their citizens problems for them. I'm wishing this shit doesn't escalate between these other people again buddy. Especially they aren't going to go unscathed again buddy. I'm making another phone call to this other associate of mine. I'm prompting these other aliens to return back here again buddy. I'm waiting for these other aliens to retrieve me. I'm going to be traveling to another Galaxy. we aren't traveling together. Buddy to another country? I'm going to be visiting this region again buddy. I'm going to be coaxing someone's else into teaching me. Because If I'm not able to communicate with them. I'm learning to use ths Spanish people vocabulary again buddy. I'm not fitting with them. Likewise, If I weren't capable of convincing anyone else that I'm being born in this specific territory. God has bestowed this green complexion upon me. Whenever I'm much younger than them. I'm not becoming another person's victim again buddy. I'm went through another freaking accident again buddy. Likewise, If I'm not capable of convincing them. I have been working with these other harmful chemicals last year again buddy? If they don't want anyone else to believe me. I wasn't able to stop these other chemicals from splashing upon my skin again buddy. Alex these other chemicals have turned my skin this complexion again buddy Joseph said. "If I wasn't capable of swaying many of those other people's opinion of me. You haven't had any sort of a negative reaction to some of these other chemical last year's again buddy. They might have thought that you are this deranged person. You're making this shit up about me. Because you're wanting to impress someone else again buddy. you aren't capable of lying to them. Because they wouldn't have wonder why you have these two-pointed ears lobes again buddy. You don't look like them. you're playing the role of this character Spock. Who has appeared in this television show. I believe that this shows was called Star galactic war again buddy" Alex said. "Who is this person? I never heard of this gentleman. I haven't been watching any of these other television episodes yet again buddy." Joseph said.

## The Speech

*Joseph was trying to convince this woman. Steve was trying to insult her. (5 years)*

Joseph was going to be describing this young lady's appearance to these other people. This young lady is very captivating to these two gentlemen. This young lady was discussing something else with these two gentlemen. These two people are behaving badly around this young woman. This young lady wasn't able to compliment these two gentlemen. This young lady isn't going to be able to spell this other person's name correctly again, fellas. This lady wasn't living near both of these other people. Steve has been given this remarkable eyesight according to everyone else. Steve is having to deal with these other matters himself. Steve was unaware of this young lady's presence there again folks. Steve was going to be expressing his own beliefs with these other people. Steve was going to be trying to pursue another career. Steve wants to become a firefighter. Steve does possess this other wide range of skills again, fellas. These two people are very dashing to everyone else. Steve has been feeling very valuable around these two people. These other firefighters have been playing another significant role in our society. "If you weren't doing anything else to help these two people. Because you're going to be able to use some sort of animal magnetism against these other people's wives. So you're going to be trying to attract these other women" Alex said. "Did anyone else notice these two people," Steve said. "I'm not going to be describing this young lady's face to anyone else. This young lady is almost around five feet inches tall again buddy. This young lady is wearing this blue colored dress again fellas. This young lady was wearing these other pairs of high heels shoes upon her feet" Joseph said. "This young lady has been applying an extra layer of this red-colored lipstick to both of her lips again buddy. This young lady has very wavy hair again fellas. this young lady's hair is flowing down past her butthole? If this young woman isn't going to be trying to fondle me. If she isn't going to be flirting with these other gentlemen" Steve said. "OK, I'm going to be trying to remain calm about it again, buddy," Joseph said. "I'm not sure if this young lady is very lovely again, fellas. You didn't have to try to agree with these two gentlemen. If I'm not sure if I'm giving anyone else an accurate description of this young lady's facial features again fellas. this woman is a very seductive person. I'm going to be able to enjoy myself. because this young lady is the object of these other gentlemen's desires again, buddy. This woman is wearing a very lovely bracelet around her ankle again, fellas. this young lady's breasts are enormous compared to everyone else. I'm not sure if this young lady's breasts could have melted another stick of that butter. I'm going to be trying to shovel a small percentage of this young lady's breasts into my mouth again fella. This young woman's breasts are looking very tasty to everyone else. I'm not going to be making any sort of comparison between these two ladies' breast sizes. I'm taking another glance down at this young woman's ass cheeks. If you aren't going to be trying to grab ahold of this young lady's ass cheeks. before I'm going to be able to reach the top of this mountain. I'm going to be placing both of my strong hands into this young lady's other small creases again fella. I'm going to be hanging onto this young lady's breasts again buddy. I'm going to be taking advantage of my other opportunity again buddy. Because I'm not sure if this lady's breasts are the same size as the Empire State Building. I'm going to become the next King of the jungle. Whenever I'm getting to devour this young lady's ass cheeks again, fella. I'm going to be ripping off this young lady's jeans with the force of my set of teeth. Because I'm going to be feeling like I'm becoming this caged animal. I'm going to be setting this small animal free from these other sets of restraints again, fella. So this animal can be running amongst its other male counterparts again, fellas," Steve said. "I'm not sure if you might have found this other shit very nasty to you. I'm much older than these other women" Alex said. "this young lady is going to be resembling another young feline. Maybe I shouldn't have been able to be chatting with someone else about these other women. I'm going to want someone else to provide me and my friend with this young lady's cellphone number again, buddy. I'm not sure if I'm going to be able to call upon this young lady" Alex said. "If you aren't going to be able to chat with us. I might have wanted another person to introduce my other friends to their other female acquaintances. Because I'm going to be getting to know them. If you aren't hurrying up again fella. we aren't very interesting to these other people again fella. I'm going to be trying to fondle this young lady's large breasts again, buddy. I'm not letting another person be fleeing the scene of the crime. I'm not letting another person be wasting my precious time again, fella. If this young woman isn't capable of responding to another person's question about her life. this young lady shouldn't have been looking for another hobby again fella. So these two people can do this other stuff again fellas. This young woman might have been dating one of these other two gentlemen. I'm not going to be getting another hands-on experience with these other women. If I'm going to be dragging another person into my bedroom. I'm not sure if I'm capable of ripping off another person's panties for them. I'm going to be trying to fuck with these two people." Steve said. Joseph was going to be trying to walk towards anyone else. what are these people talking about amongst themselves? "I'm not going to be letting any of these other people do anything to another person. If you aren't capable of doing anything about it again buddy. You aren't going to be messing with these other people. If these other people are standing in front of you" Alex said. Steve is going to be trying to manipulate these other people. Because Steve is wanting to try to fuck several of these other ladies. Steve might have seen this lady's very large breasts again folks. Steve has been able to convince himself. She should have let some of these other doctors to be performing another breast enlargement surgery on herself. Steve also has been able to convince this young lady. She should have been able to get in contact with him. This young lady wasn't another very attractive person. Steve has told this young lady. She has this very smelly breath again fellas. If this young lady wasn't able to listen to this other gentleman insulting her again, fellas. This young lady has been trying to slap the shit out of this man. Alex is going to be trying to defend this young lady's honor for her again fellas. Steve wasn't trying to convince this young lady. She has this very stinky pussy again folks. Steve wouldn't have been able to say any of this other shit to this young lady's face. this young person is a very classy lady. Steve doesn't have any of these other charming personality traits again fellas.

Steve isn't another very caring person. "I'm not going to be attempting to persuade this young lady to remove her pairs of panties for me. I'm not sure if these other people find this other shit very obvious to themselves. Someone might have blessed this young lady with these other whore like a tendency, in my opinion, again, buddy," Alex said. "I want to try to stick my penis inside of this young lady's anus cavity again, fella? What if I'm capable of doing this other stuff properly again, buddy? I'm not sure if I'm going to be qualified to apply for this person's job again, buddy," Steve said, " I'm not going to be allowing another person to be saying anything horrible about these other people's families. Steve wasn't able to convince these other people. Because Steve isn't capable of trying to fuck this young lady's brain out of her head again fella," Joseph said. " Steve is being another asshole. I'm not sure if this other person is going to be kicking this guy's ass again fella? So I'm going to be trying to confront this other gentleman" this woman said. "No, I'm not sure if you're allowed to be doing this other stuff to these other agents. I'm not familiar with this other person's Position again sweetheart. I'm not allowing another person to be touching anyone else. Because Steve is an employee. This man could have been arrested for sexually harassing another person again, sweetheart. Because if you aren't sure if you should have been able to assault this other federal employee. I'm not sure if you should have been near these other gentlemen. if I'm not going to be given this guy another piece of my mind," Joseph said. So this young woman is going to be walking toward these two agents. Steve wasn't there by himself. "You weren't saying these other terrible things about anyone else. I'm not some huge slut. I'm not sure if you haven't noticed these other things about myself. I might have these two very enormous ass cheeks again fella. If you're going to be trying to bend my body over this very large desk. So you're going to try to fuck me. But you shouldn't have been referring to anyone else as some other person's whore. If you're going to be using my other friends as some of these other sexual objects again, sweetheart. I'm not sure if another person should have been using any of those condoms again fella. I'm not letting another person be using my other friends as some human display case," This woman said. This woman was slapping this other guy in his face again fellas. "This person is going to become the manager of another McDonald's. He was wondering if they could use this slogan in one of their company television commercials. I'm not sure what you're going to be saying to me. Are you capable of defending yourself? I'm not sure if this stuff isn't true about yourself. I want someone else to convince me. You weren't saying this other horrible

*Hillary radell was upon the stage. She was trying to give a speech folks. (5 years)*

They think these documents belong to an agent. They weren't taking it away from them. Joseph is laying those documents on this lady's desk. Joseph was reading it again folks. Because Joseph is going to be using the information against them. Someone else has marked this material classified again fellas. Hillary was standing on the stage. Hillary was going to be reading her speech to them. They're going to be attending this special event. Hillary has been able to convince herself. Hillary is a very valuable asset to these other people. Because Hillary has these other political aspirations in the future. Whenever she was a very young person. Someone else has been the inspiration for this person wanting to lead this nation. Hillary wasn't making any strides in achieving her other dreams. Hillary wanted to become the next president of the United States. If Hillary isn't interested in making this other decision for herself. Hillary was a Harvard University graduate. Hillary was fabricating these other things about herself. Hillary has been waiting to add many of these other intriguing details about herself. Hillary was having these other sick fantasies about having sexual interactions with many of these gentlemen. Hillary wasn't based this shit on any other truthful life scenarios again, fellas. Hillary isn't a very business-like person. Hillary had been working with these other employees in this other variety of companies throughout her lifetime. Hillary is a very cunning woman. Hillary enjoyed degrading her staff. Hillary was coercing these other gentlemen into doing these other horrible things to them. Because if Hillary wasn't able to convince these men herself. They would have lost their interest in this lady. they wouldn't have been able to vote for this lady in the upcoming elections. Hillary was going to try to inform these other voters. They shouldn't have believed any of these other reporters. Especially if these reporter were writing something cheesey about their favorite candidate. Especially if they were going to be presenting this lady's husband's past transgressions to them. "Joseph there isn't any chance of these other people getting this woman elected as the president of the United States of America. They weren't taken my prediction very lightly again buddy. If they can't imagine this stuff happening to their favorite candidate. Hillary isn't taking this country in another whole new direction. If Hillary is jeopardizing our nation's security again fellas. They weren't utilizing some of these tools in their arsenal. Whenever they're dealing with another major catastrophe event. If Hillary is going to be solving our country's economic crisis in another entire year. Hillary was going to be fighting against us. Hillary is ruining these other people's lives. If these other people weren't successful during their lifetime. Clifford wasn't going to be contributing his money to his wife's political campaign. "If these other people are impacting this country economic growth again buddy. I wasn't spiritual evolving in these past few years. We weren't interested in facing these other serious challenges in our lives. Hillary haven't been providing these other senators with any incentive to improve upon our country's financial services. They must try to preserve their citizen's quality of life. If they were going to be helping us. We mustn't provide these other foreign leaders with other financial support again fella. if we're not making this shit another group efforts again fella. They were affecting these other citizen's sovereignty. We shouldn't have been dependent upon these people. if these politicians aren't going to be held responsible for creating this financial crisis to begin with in the past few decades. These politicians haven't been able to get their law bypass the house of Congress. Theses politicians doesn't have any other economic plans for the foreseeable future. If they weren't being another hindrance to the progression of this country. Clifford has built an alliance with these other foreign leaders. Whenever Clifford has been sharing his wife other ideas with them. Clifford has been making these other improvements within our banking systems. I'm not going to be capable of having many of these other strange visions of mine. This country has a very bright future ahead of itself. I'm trying to implement many of my other goals into our country's foreign policy. So I can build another bridge. I'm going to be taking possession of these other foreign country's resources again fellas. So I'm going to be continuing to strengthen our relationship with these other foreign leaders. I don't have a good rapport with these other politicians. I'm not going to be playing another significant role into the lives of our citizens. So If I'm not able to move my wife's agenda forward again fellas. If I'm not explaining these other things to my supporters. If folks' there isn't something greater for everyone else over the horizon. I'm going to be persevering this country's global dominance. I'm going to be securing my place within our children history books. I'm going to be attempting to balance this country's budget. I'm not letting another major financial catastrophe to happened to us. if these other politicians have these other poor leadership skills again fellas. Because if these other politicians can't find a way of fixing the rapid decline of these other people's morals. I'm not going to be allowing another person to suffering because of these other politicians policies. these other politicians have been making these similar mistakes over the past few decades. But I wasn't anticipating this shit would have been happening to us. Because these other politicians weren't capable of developing their political strategy again fellas. if this previous president's plan isn't going to be working in our citizen's favor anytime soon fellas. I'm not going to be abandoning our own founding father's principles. I'm not sure if I'm capable of changing this country foreign policy again fellas. Fellas Theses other politicians are affecting our country's educational system. I'm not going to be hiring these other politicians. If these teachers weren't capable of teaching these politicians. How to connect the dots again fellas. If these teachers aren't meeting the educational needs of their other students. if they aren't willing to adopt my other beliefs again fellas. Because They weren't interested in meeting these other schools' broad requirements again fellas. If they weren't accepting these other students into those other educational programs in the future. They aren't contributing anything of their to theses other educational programs. if these other teachers aren't capable of teaching their other students the proper school curriculum again, folks. They weren't interested in doing these other basic math equations again folks. we must lend these other people's children a helping hand in the future. if folks' our country's founding fathers have established the rules of this country. I'm not going to become a developer. I'm not going to be capable of manufacturing these items for these other politicians. So these other people can try to use these products in the future. I'm not sure if these other foreign leaders are capable of exporting these items to our country. I'm making sure our country will remain independent again, folks. I'm going to be stabilizing the growth of this country. I'm offering these other CEOs an opportunity for growth and other manufacturing opportunities. I'm not sure if they would've given someone else a chance to reform our country's financial institutions. If we're allowing these foreign adversaries to dictate our country's plan to us. I'm not sure How we're conducting our business with these overseas companies. If we're letting these other leadership to bully us. If we don't create a new agenda ourselves. I haven't failed yet. I'm going to be delivering on my other promises to you. we aren't stuck in this moment. I'm going to be introducing this new regulation to everyone else. I'm going to the House of Congress. I'm finding other ways of cutting costs for the citizens of this country. So I'm not depending on anyone else to invest their money into these other technical advances again, folks. I'm going to be attempting to fund this laboratory. So they can continue to do their research into artificial intelligence. They can do their stem cell research again, folks. I'm going to be able to solve our country's problems again, folks. They aren't capable of accomplishing anything for anyone else. These teachers haven't properly trained them. So I'm not sure if we should financially support them. I'm a woman. I'm attempting to rule this world. I'm going to be accomplishing my mission with this iron fist again folk. I'm going to be using a firm handshake with them. They wouldn't have put anyone else in charge of these other people's children's lives. I'm your leader. I'm sharing with you and these other people some exciting news right now. I'm going to be implementing this plan of mine. You won't find it exciting to you. I'm not sure if I have developed this revolutionary approach to fixing the structure of our country. They have advised me. I mustn't attempt to restore our citizen's freedom to them. I have a revolutionary idea in my mind. I have created a program. I have been working alongside these great people on some of these other Country issues for a long time. I have been working with someone else on another project of mine. I'm incorporating it into my other goals in the future. if we could've been experimenting on these people. If we could have developed a drug to heal them. I'm not sure who has created a deadly virus folks. People are getting sick because of it. I'm making sure these scientists find a cure for this virus. So I'm going to make sure that we are capable of safeguarding our children against the effects of the virus. Once they have found a cure for this epidemic. I'm going to be offering many of these other people these incentives to take advantage of this medical breakthrough folks. I'm putting forth my effort to follow the rules of law again folks. I'm not sure if I'm capable of accomplishing this task myself. I'm to revise our abortion laws myself. So we can benefit from it right away fellows. I can attempt to amend the entire constitution of the United States of America folks. We can revise many parts of the United States Constitution. I can pass more laws folks. I can try to expand the size of our country's military folks. I can try to change this country.

*They was discussing about how the guy wife injured her back amongst themselves. (5 years)*

Alex told him. He believed it was related to something else folks. This guy is sitting behind a very large desktop. Alex would've preferred to be linked to someone else. They share similar characteristics alike, Selena Gomez. The young lady can handle herself. This lady is currently under a lot of pressure herself. This lady might've been an old person. Alex's mind is consumed with these other vivid fantasies of this lady. They're sharing an intimate moment. What if this stuff happened to this lady during their sexual encounter again folks? This lady could've sustained an injury herself. Alex doesn't feel like inflicting pain on this lady's body. What if they're having these other orgasms together? Alex is being truthful with this lady. Alex has been attractive to this lady. Alex has observed a stark contrast between himself and this famous poet. Alex made it clear to this young lady. He's not changing his name to the nickname symbolic poet 20. Alex has been observing this young lady for a while now. this lady has this deep admiration for this poet. Alex has been having other explicit fantasies about themselves. Specifically, Alex imagines this young lady spreading both of her legs apart for him. Alex wants to try to kiss this young lady's thighs again folks. the Janitor was fucking this woman? Alex doesn't want this young lady fucking someone else. Alex is unsure if this young lady can properly perform those types of sexual positions with him. What If she doesn't feel comfortable being around him? If she is struggling with her sexuality again folks. I'm suggesting other stuff to most of my other readers. this woman should've been reading a sex manual. Alex is expecting this young lady to lie there motionless beside him. Joseph frequently uses these derogatory comments to characterize this young woman's behavior against folks. Joseph wants someone else to tell it to this young lady's face. The young lady's identity remains unknown to them. They're attempting to speculate on this young lady's name again folks. Alex is going to try to obtain this young lady's telephone number from someone else. "I don't agree with you. Alex this woman is having these other weird sexual fantasies about you. you're not having sexual intimacy with this guy's wifey again buddy? Alex this woman is engaging in sex with them. Alex this lady has done this shit with these people on different occasions again buddy" Joseph said. Alex is staring at this guy's eye socket again folks. " I'm not having any sort of resentment towards you. If you're ruining my wife's reputation amongst these peers of mine" this guy said. "If you're hurrying up again buddy. I'm not getting into trouble because of you. I shouldn't have returned to this hotel again buddy. So I'm staying off of my two feet now buddy. I'm lying down on the couch awhile again buddy. I'm enjoying my moment alone again buddy. I'm not serving time in jail because of you. If you can't understand my position on this issue again buddy. If you're not going to listen to me. I'm giving everyone else some valuable insight into women's sexuality again buddy" this guy said. "They're not wanting anyone else looking at their spouse's bodies anymore buddy. You should've known better again buddy. If these women are lying motionless on a very soft bed frame. If you don't ask this lady politely again buddy. If she is letting someone fuck her again buddy. If you're lying beside this woman. if this lady is looking pretty miserable again buddy. If she has a miserable excuse for a husband. If this woman can't stand being near him. This woman must've been having other nightmares about this guy's small penis again buddy. They have these very small penises themselves. if they're measuring the size of their penises themselves. If they're sticking their penises into his girlfriend's uterus again buddy. you wouldn't prevent this catastrophe event from happening to them. if he's climbing on top of this young lady again buddy. this guy must've weighed almost five hundred pounds again buddy. If you're putting this woman's body in a different position now again buddy. If you're preventing this lady from moving around again buddy. If she doesn't want to be with him. If they're jamming their small penis into this guy's wife's uterus again buddy. If I'm not able to ensure them. They're not getting hurt while having sex with their husband" Alex said. "She is still coping with her problems again buddy. This lady's mother-in-law must've persuaded her to remain married to her son. He must've been this miserable slob again buddy" Joseph said. Alex was getting in touch with them. This specific person has been working for a specific cab company? While they're finding solutions to their problems again folks. they wouldn't been able to fix it themselves? whenever the manager has sent his workers to meet with them. " I'm not this person. Who is supposed to be driving these two people to the airport? They're expecting someone else to be picking you up again fellows," this cab driver said. "Yes, We're these two people. you came to pick up here again fellow," Alex said. They're climbing into the back seat of this guy's automobile. this taxi cab driver needs to identify them. Because he has been feeling curious about it again folks. If they didn't meet them. " you mustn't know anything else about us" Alex said. "Fellas it's nice to meet you. I could swear to myself. I might've known it again buddy" this guy said. "You must get straight to the point again fellows. If you're frustrated with me. We're not exactly alike again buddy" Joseph said.

*They've returned to the scene of the crime today's folks. (5 years)*

Folks It has been over a year. since they were last home. They are now determined to make better decisions for themselves. They have been disappointed with the outcomes of their own attempts again folks. They have experienced confusion once more folks. They did not anticipate their inability to succeed independently themselves. Alex was staring at this other guy's face again folks. Alex is puzzled by this little green creature inability to generate his own ideas again folks. they have exhausted all their other options themselves. They find themselves. Folks back at square one nowadays. They are brainstorming and devising strategies independently themselves. I think that these two guys goal is to enhance their plans moving forward again ladies and gentlemen. Alex has been determined to avoid being perceived as incompetent once more folks. Alex has been actively attempting to acquire two passports for their own use again folks. they are unable to leave the country without them. Alex thinks that It is imperative that they possess these two passports. whenever they are traveling abroad. "I'm thinking about trying to hold onto it again buddy?" Alex said. Alex is perplexed by the repeated instances of this small green creature approaching children. Joseph purpose behind its actions remains unclear to his friend. "I've believed that this little boy was selling those other people theses cups of lemonade beverages again buddy? I've believed that this little boy was standing nearby an train station again buddy" Joseph said. " If you're not curious about if two of those passports are legitimate again buddy. Because I've believed that this little boy is using some worthless material again buddy. I'm not sure, who's the one that has been able to manufacture this material again buddy. You didn't want to inspect the material. So you can see if any of this other material was of the highest quality in my opinion again buddy. Before you've decided that you would've went ahead with this financial transaction again buddy. Whoever this person's child is in my opinion again buddy. They should've tried to hire an expert again buddy. So he could've been examining many of those other items himself. I'm not sure, if I'm your other identical twin in my opinion again buddy. Did you think that you could've trusted him? You should've been given the same opportunities as anyone else in my opinion again buddy. Because I'm thinking about providing you with some of my own input buddy. Whenever Joseph it comes to this type of other serious legal matter again buddy. you didn't try to ask me. If I known Joseph this other person's child name again buddy?" Alex said. "I'm not doing anything else for you. whenever we're entering into the lobby of an local airport in my opinion again buddy. If they don't inquire about the legitimacy of those two documents in my opinion again buddy. I'm wondering why wouldn't you get some of our own funds back from him" Alex said. "What were you expect to receive back from this little boy's in my opinion again buddy? You're not receiving an handshake from this little boy's in my opinion again buddy. If you didn't noticed that this little boy's is acting a little suspicious again buddy. You're not convincing me. I've believed that this little boy's isn't allowing you to make any of your own decisions in my opinion again buddy. I've believed that this little boy's didn't force you, or anyone else to go through with it in my opinion again buddy" Alex said. " If this little boy was about to try to defraud you. If you're not going to be able to describe this little boy's appearance to me. If I was wanting to talk to him" Alex said." I've believed that this little boy's name is Little Rome," Joseph said. Alex was smirking once in a while again folks. Alex did want to try to question him. I've believed that any of those other women's. Who is trying to give birth to any of those other children in my opinion again folks. I've believed that this child parent's has been given the responsibility in accordance to the law of any particular state that she been given the rights to give this particular child an name in my opinion again folks. This woman isn't trying to raise some other woman's child in my opinion again folks. Was this lady expecting that she would've been raising an con-artist sometime later in her own life again buddy" Joseph said. "why wouldn't we continue to allow this other stuff to happen to them. you might've been able to persude this little boy's mother to go out romantic date with you. I've believed that this woman could've been another citizens of some other foreign country in my opinion again buddy. if you're going to be moving to another foreign country. So you could've tried to join another country's military service in my opinion again buddy. They're trying to force many of theses other soldiers to travel overseas somewhere again buddy. So they're going to want to try to invaded another foreign country in my opinion again buddy" Joseph said. "I'm not asking you. what you're trying to say to me. I'm getting sick of dealing with this other bullshit in my opinion again buddy. I've been partaking in some of these others different things as of late in my opinion again buddy. I've been creating my very own to-do list in my opinion again buddy. I'm trying to complete it, as we're speaking about it in my opinion again buddy. Whenever I'm visiting another friend's of mine. Yes, I do have these other skills set in my own opinion again buddy. I do have the ability of becoming very successful in this day and age in my opinion again buddy. whenever I'm working on any of my other projects in my opinion again buddy. Whenever I'm putting in some of my own efforts in my opinion again buddy" Alex said. Alex was looking into different direction in my opinion again folks. "You're not an very good comedian in my opinion again buddy. I've believed that no one else would've believed that those two passports were legitimates documents in my opinion again buddy. You didn't try to check out the material in my opinion again buddy. if you're going to try to buy two authentic passports in my opinion again buddy. If you couldn't spot the flaws within the fabric of the materials in my opinion again buddy. whenever we're thinking about returning there ourselves. If you happen to see it in my opinion again buddy. If someone else is standing in front of this service counter in my opinion again buddy. If this person doesn't have any question about the legitimacy of thoses other two documents in my opinion again buddy. If they don't suspect that we're doing anything wrong in my opinion again buddy. If an custom agent doesn't confront us. If any of those other custom agent doesn't doubt the legitimacy of thoses two other document in my opinion again buddy. I've believed that they shouldn't have tried to deport us. But just in case that they're going to try to transport us back to our own province. They would've been trying to placed us inside of a prison system again buddy?" Alex said. "you can rest assured that you might've made the right decision for yourself. I didn't see any sort of these other problems happening between the two of us. I didn't want to try to purchase two of those passports from this little boy again buddy" Joseph said. "I'm making sure that I'm collecting some sort of proof of this little boy's illegal misconduct in my opinion again buddy. Especially if I'm going to be presenting it to those other judges that are in a courthouse again buddy. I wasn't expecting that you're going to try to buy any of these other worthless documents from him. If this person was someone else like us. I believe that this person would've gotten into some sort of serious trouble with the local authorities in my opinion again buddy. I've believed that this little boy had someone else. who could've been trying to work alongside him? If they weren't allowing us, the opportunity that we need to try to gain some sort of access to several of those other documents in my opinion again buddy. If they're not trying to investigate any of this other shit that these other people have been trying to do to us? I've believed a woman named Hillary Randall. If Hillary doesn't need to attend this conference herself?" Alex said. "Hillary is being put on this schedule in my opinion again buddy. So Hillary is going to have to be there in attendance in my opinion again buddy. Hillary is giving another speech in front of a massive crowd of people again buddy. I believe that this event is going to be held somewhere in Los Angeles California again today buddy. I believe it would've been almost six months ago in my opinion again buddy. I haven't had the chance to try to write down anything else about it myself. Hillary isn't making a fool of me. Because Hillary does deserve this shit in my opinion again buddy. I'm getting revenge very soon in my opinion again buddy. Because I'm not some village idiot in my opinion anymore buddy. I'm going to try to fuck this lady's daughter in my opinion again buddy" Joseph said. " I don't want to see anything terrible happening to another member of this lady's family. If you're trying to fuck this lady's daughter in the pussy again buddy" Alex said. " I didn't try to partake in any type of other sexual activities with this specific lady's daughter nowadays buddy. I'm not letting you. Joseph or someone else is on a secret of mine. If you would've been trying to help me. But you didn't want to get ball-deep into this woman's pussy in my opinion again buddy" Joseph said. Joseph wasn't laughing along with another friend of his in my opinion again folks. " you didn't need to fuck this woman's grandma again buddy. I want to know, why I would've had this silly little grin upon my face in my opinion again buddy?" Alex said.

" I don't have time to go through this shit again buddy. I haven't done some of those other things to this lady's daughter in my opinion again buddy. I wasn't able to avoid it myself. Did he mention this other shit to you? whoever this other person is in my opinion again buddy. I believe that this person could've been another staff member of their agency in my opinion again buddy. If they're another member of the law enforcement community again buddy. If I believed that this person was trying to gather this other evidence against both of us. If I've believed that we're going to try to use those two fake passports ourselves. So if you're expecting that we're going to be able to try to sneak into this other foreign country again buddy. I'm not going to try to pursue this worthless plan of yours in my opinion again buddy. I'm thinking that I should've been trying to finish it nowadays again buddy" Alex said. they were walking toward this customer service counter in my opinion again folks. " I'm expecting that you're going to allow me. Friend to try to speak with an employee of this establishment again buddy. I'm visiting this very fine country in my opinion again buddy. I need to try to get my, and my mother's Friend one of those other temporary green cards in my opinion again buddy. So if you're thinking that you should've been trying to help me?" Joseph said. I've believed some very tall man. Who is sitting behind this very large desktop again folks? This guy was looking straight at the both of them. " I could've been trying to assist you" this employee said. They're offering this guy's two of those other passports in my opinion again folks. Whenever this guy did try to examine it himself. This employees hasn't found anyIt of other flaws within the material of two of those guy's passport again folks. " I've believed that everything else does seem to be in it's own proper order in my opinion again todays. You're going to be able to try to speak with an custom agent very soon again folks. So I'm sending them, right now to the proper department today. So you could've tried to receive two of those green card for yourselves" this employee said that shit to them. If they don't receive two of those temporary visa card themselves. Then they couldn't become an citizens of this foreign country in my opinion again buddy. Because if they're expecting to obtain some type of official citizenship in my opinion again folks. So they could've stayed within the parameters of this other country in my opinion again folk. They're not going to allowed these other two illegal immigrants to cross over the borders into this other country in my opinion again folks. "You can't let some of these illegal immigrants spread this Ebola virus amongst these other citizens in my opinion again buddy. Whenever they're coming here to visit this beautiful countryside in my opinion again buddy. I believe that this land belongs to those other ancestors of mine. I've believed that they might've fought the enemies for me and my children in my opinion again buddy. They were trying to preserve our founding fathers' legacy for me and my other friends and relatives in my opinion again buddy" this employee said. "I wouldn't have let most of those other illegal immigrants run completely free amongst these other people in my opinion again buddy. If you're not able to keep tabs on the whereabouts of those other illegal immigrants again buddy. I'm trying to explain this stuff to you. before I'm leaving this fucking establishment in my opinion again fellow. They shouldn't have allowed those other illegal immigrants to be fucking any of these other men's wives again fellow. I don't want two of those illegal immigrants to be spreading their terrible virus to someone's else spouse again buddy. I don't want any of those other illegal immigrants to try to fuck my wife again fellow. You might've been passing this guy's wife along some highway again buddy. If you're going to try to fuck my friend's wife again fellows. You might've been trying to do this guy's wife a huge favor in my opinion again buddy. So Im not fucking this woman's in my opinion anymore buddy" this guy said.

## The Prison Prophet

*They were going to try to board the aircraft themselves, folks. (5 years)*

Joseph is fighting with his friend. Joseph doesn't want anyone else moving with him and his friend to the Russian Federation. Alex was ignoring him. Because he doesn't agree with his friend. Joseph has these other preferences for his own life. Alex is dealing with his friend's behavior again folks. Alex is concerned about his friend's future. Joseph doesn't consent to moving forward in the future. "I'm not going to be showing my face to them," Joseph said. "If they aren't permitting me and my friend to return to this country. Alex wanted someone else to forge his birth certificate for him. Alex has thought about it again folks. They're visiting their relatives. They're thinking when the dust has settled down again folks. Alex doesn't think any of this other stuff is feasible for him. "I'm going to be purchasing these fake birth certificates for us. I'm using these fake birth certificates myself. I'm hoping that there aren't any of those other foolish people living amongst us" Alex said. Alex was embarking on this journey. Alex was creating this whole new identity for himself. "Hillary isn't expecting this stuff to happen to them. Hillary isn't capable of explaining many of these other things to her own husband's associates again buddy?" Joseph said. Hillary wasn't capable of redeeming herself. Hillary was able to establish a connection between them. If Hillary isn't capable of mending many of her other ways of doing these things again folks. Joseph was waiting for someone else to take the initiative between themselves. If Hillary isn't capable of rectifying her other actions herself. Joseph wants someone else to be able to dismantle this lady's credibility among themselves. Alex was able to give these other people his perspective on this topic again folks. Joseph doesn't believe in this stuff himself. Joseph is working to tarnish this woman's reputation amongst these other people in the business world. Joseph has been wanting him and his friend to be able to seize control of this entire planet. "Then I'm adding many of those other things to my to-do list again buddy. Hillary shouldn't have been bothering me. if Hillary doesn't send someone else to fucked with us. I'm not going to be able to promise you. Hillary is going to regret it again buddy. Hillary is a scumbag. They weren't being respectful of them. I'm not entrusting these other people with my sanity again buddy" Joseph said. Joseph has walked into a different place. Joseph is packing up his other personal belongings again folks. So he can place this stuff into a very large suitcase. They were going to be arriving at the airport. They were going to be boarding this aircraft. So they were going to be traveling across these other international borders. Joseph was saying these other harsh things about his friends. "I'm not capable of reassuring you. I'm not capable of venting my other frustrations with you. I might have some resentment towards them. Because they were physically abusing me. I'm not capable of slandering someone's else name again buddy. I'm not capable of harboring any animosity toward them. If I'm coming with you. I'm not this very patriotic person," Joseph exclaimed. I'm not sure if this story isn't over between them. I'm going to be telling everyone else about them.

## *They're discussing their plans for extortion this lady family again folk. (5 years)*

"this person has been harming them. They're facing these other serious repercussions again folks. You shouldn't have done anything foolish to them" Alex said. "I'm not explaining this stuff to you. You couldn't have injured them. I'm not going to be defeating them. You aren't capable of overcoming these obstacles again buddy" Joseph said. "If they aren't going to be catching us? They're gathering this other evidence against us. What If they were able to convict us? We aren't capable of conspiring against them? This old person has been telling me. If you aren't capable of making something of yourself. I'm not taking advantage of them. If you aren't capable of preparing for this stuff again buddy. If you aren't capable of neutralizing them. Because you have a lot of this discord in your own life. if you're allowing these things to escalate between yourselves. If you aren't striving to maximize your potential in this world. Nobody else is doing this stuff to you. So if you aren't capable of blackmailing them. I'm not going to be doing anything wrong to them. If these people aren't giving my friend the maximum amount of prison time again buddy. I'm not sure what they're thinking about again buddy. I'm not allowing anyone else to be blackmailing this lady's relative again buddy. I'm not sure if I'm receiving a fifty-year jail sentence again buddy. They might have been condemning us. You are responsible for persuading me. I'm not going to go along with my friend's plan again buddy. I'm not letting anyone else be dragging everyone else into this equation with them. Because if they aren't holding someone else liable for their criminal offense again buddy. I'm not allowing anyone else to determine my fate for me. I'm not sure why we're discussing this subject amongst ourselves. if they aren't capable of verifying this information for me. They are connected to this other government official. Hillary doesn't want anyone else to be associated with us. They were being employed by the Department of Justice? they weren't being very supportive of me. Hillary was doing this stuff to her other associates throughout her political campaign" Alex said. "I'm not going to be thinking about them and their nonsense again buddy. They aren't capable of convicting us. Because Hillary is lying to them. They might have wanted someone else to donate their own money to this woman's political campaign. If someone else isn't helping me. Whenever I'm trying to verify any portion of this woman's information with them. I'm shedding light on them. I'm thinking that there is corruption running through the halls of Congress. If I'm not persuading them. They should have been reopening their investigation into these other crimes that someone else has been committing over the past several years again buddy. If I'm not investigating this shit myself. I'm going to be searching for them. You're not intimidating to me" Joseph said. "They aren't burying this evidence somewhere else again buddy. Especially if we're not able to convince them. if Hillary is getting involved with them. They're not exposing them" Alex said. "I'm not letting these other people know that I'm an alien. I'm not another human being. So I'm not getting this shit through my friend's skull again buddy. Why you're not referring to me? As an adult. But I'm not such a scary creature. I'm not living on this planet. Especially if you're speaking with me. You're being extremely rude towards me. They haven't been providing these people with this false information about me. What if Alex this shit isn't true about me" Joseph said. "You're not going to be getting rid of me. Because I'm making these important decisions on my behalf. If I'm not reaching out to them. You're not worrying about me. I don't know what buddy my nationality is nowadays" Alex said. "I'm going to be coming to someone else galaxy again buddy. You're a real jackass. Nobody else has sent me. I'm not sure if I'm going to be familiar with the state of Oregon. I'm not allowing this shit to bother me. I'm making another decision on my own friend's behalf" Joseph said. "I don't believe them. They haven't gained access to this information themselves? If Hillary doesn't figure this stuff out herself. I'm not responsible for stealing those documents again buddy. I'm hacking into this governmental agency database again buddy. I'm getting access to these other people's files again buddy? I'm not threatening our nation's sovereignty again buddy. If they were going to be arresting us. if we're extorting them. they might've been considering if they should've been filing a complaint against us. I'm involved in this other illegal practice with him. I'm thinking that they are considering if they want to change me and my friend with committing a felony in this case again buddy. If you haven't heard about any of these other state laws" Alex said. " I'm not a foolish person," Joseph said.

## *I do believe this gentleman is a witch fellows. (5 years)*

Joseph was taking those photographs of this man's spouse again folks. This man has informed them. he will be reporting these two fugitive to someone else. Joseph was stating his intention to them. Joseph is capable of providing this reporter with these photos of them. Joseph was doing these other things to them. Alex hasn't seen photos of this woman's body yet again folks. If they aren't going to be blackmailing them. Alex has been experiencing himself these other series of events. They almost got away with it again folks. Alex isn't capable of facing any of these other repercussions himself. Alex thinks the statute of limitations had already expired on him. They weren't capable of filing out their claim against them. they were expecting these two fugitive to be able to achieve this stuff within an specific timeframe again folks. So someone else can file an restraining order against them. Joseph was touching this woman's legs again folks. If Alex doesn't intervene on this woman's behalf. Joseph was acting inappropriately towards them. "Nobody else wouldn't have caught both of us. Whenever I'm committing this other crime alongside you. I'm sitting inside of an huge stadium. I'm attending another Britney's Faith concert" Alex said. "why I'm not going to be talking to you? Because I don't know anything about them. Alex this shit isn't true about them. You aren't smarter than me. I'm not allowing anyone else to do anything else for me. you are full of this horse shit again buddy. I'm not capable of spreading these other diseases amongst them. I'm not capable of interacting with you. If they were capable of repeating this same ole stuff themselves. How did they come up with this shit themselves? They might have been imagining it themselves. If you're capable of giving someone else an wedgie again buddy. If our savior is sending you and me these other miracle again buddy. If you're going to be performing these magic tricks on me" Alex said. Alex must've overheard these two people talking about them. "you are an idiot" Joseph said. "I'm not offering you and this guy an ride in this vehicle again buddy," this man said. "If you could have been stopping me. I'm defending myself," Alex said. "you are such an witchy person," Peter said. " I'm not insulting anyone's else family. You would have found out about it from me. They were making this other stuff rough on me" Joseph said.

## Alex wanted to have sex with this call girl. (5 years)

Alex walked unannounced on these two people. They were alone together in this apartment. Joseph has been lying alongside this escort. They were sleeping with each other again fellas. Alex was trying to leave this room. These two people were having unprotected sex together. Joseph's behavior was becoming inappropriate to his friend. Alex wasn't trying to participate with these two people in this sort of sexual encounter again fellas. The escort was trying to perform oral sex on this creature. Alex was feeling very uneasy about seeing this creature in this uncompromising position with this escort. Alex isn't risking his health to try to satisfy another person's sexual needs again, fellas. This person could have been infected by another gentleman. Some sort of doctor might have been able to diagnose this person with these other sexually transmissible diseases again, folks. Because folks of this person had these other sexual escapades with some sort of infected whore again, fellas. Alex hasn't been trying to intrude on these two people's other sexual escapades together. Alex doesn't feel responsible for this creature's well-being again fellas. Alex has been very cautious of these two people. Joseph was going to be able to take advantage of their friendship again fellas. Alex wasn't feeling comfortable with being in another stable relationship with someone. Who is a current member of the opposite gender again, fellas? Joseph has become disobedient towards everyone else. Joseph wasn't interested in trying to mend his relationship with this young man. Joseph isn't interested in going through this situation with this young man. Alex was pleading with this creature to try to maintain this very low profile again folks. Joseph was trying to drag this young man into this turmoil with him. Alex wasn't trying to intervene on behalf of this creature. Joseph has been trying to follow through with his other disastrous plans again folks. Whenever Joseph was trying to fuck this nasty-looking prostitute? Alex was trying to keep this location a secret from everyone else. These two fugitives were discovering this stuff amongst themselves. Someone else was taking some sort of action against these two fugitives. These two fugitives had to be removed from this person's property. Alex has made these other assumptions about these other people. This manager was becoming aware of these other people's behavior again fellas. Joseph is trying to solicit these other sexual favors from another escort. Alex wasn't trying to risk his sanity again fellas. This policeman could have thrown both of these two people in a jailhouse. Alex is letting his mind become consumed with these other possibilities again, folks. This employee could have been reporting this incident to the sheriff's department. This person wasn't interested in figuring out these other significant clues for himself. If this person didn't lay both of his eyes upon these other people again. this person isn't this psychic. Alex is proclaiming that he has been able to try to develop his other psychic abilities again, fellas. Joseph's curiosity could have been heightened during these other most precious moments of the day. Joseph was trying to exploit those two people's other vulnerabilities again folks. Joseph was trying to use this young man's abilities to his benefit again, fellas? What If they didn't want to arrest them? If this policeman wasn't trying to place both of those two people in these handcuffs? Alex wasn't trying to become another sexual degenerate again fellas. Joseph has been able to evade these two policemen. Joseph has been trying to avoid these two policemen. Alex doesn't know how he can try to fix this situation between himself and his roommate. Joseph wasn't interested in paying another escort to try to perform these other services for him. Joseph wasn't interested in paying this manager. So Joseph can remain to stay in this room. Joseph wasn't interested in trying to control his other hormones again fellas. Alex isn't interested in getting acquainted with this escort. Joseph doesn't feel responsible for his guest getting out of hand again tonight. Alex isn't feeling concerned with this creature's other unusual interests in his life again, folks. Joseph's behavior is getting very perplexing to everyone else. Joseph isn't interested in trying to follow this young man's advice about how he should have been conducting himself in any sort of public setting again fellas. Joseph is getting very steadfast in trying to approach his other decisions in his life. Joseph wasn't interested in being too much confrontational with anyone else. Joseph was trying to disregard this young man's counsel. Alex wasn't going to be able to try to fix this creature's problem for him. Joseph could've benefited from trying to follow through with this young man's advice again, fellas. Joseph is trying to take advantage of another person's kind-hearted ways towards him. Joseph is refusing to follow his friend's instructions. Joseph isn't using any large portion of his brain cells to advance these other opportunities for himself. Alex wasn't conducting his life in such a professional manner again fellas. Joseph has known these three types of people again folks. Joseph was trying to do these other terrible things to these other people. Joseph doesn't try to admit his other mistakes to anyone else. these other people are out of this person's league again fellas. Joseph was using these other methods on these other people. Joseph wasn't being very supportive of this young man's long-term goals in life again, folks. Joseph wasn't interested in sneaking behind another person's back to get anything else that he had wanted to try to obtain during this past year. If Joseph was trying to go in another direction. If Joseph isn't interested in doing these other things a little differently than everyone else. Joseph wasn't sure if this stuff would have been very beneficial to him. Alex is sharing any of his other helpful advice with anyone else. Whoever this creature has come into contact with over the past few weeks. Alex has become another very successful man. "If you can try to excuse me. I'm trying to explain something else to these other people. You aren't interested in taking advantage of another person. If you have went through some of these other difficult situations within your life. If you aren't interested in processing this other information because of someone else interference with your other plans again, buddy," Alex said. Joseph has been having this reoccurring skin condition again folks. Joseph isn't willing to try to communicate with anyone else. "I'm not trying to speak to you, or anyone else about my other self interests in general again fella," this escort said. "Whoever has been diagnosed with some sort of rare skin disease again sweetheart. This person should have tried to come forward with important information again fellas. If this person has any sort of moral left again fellas" this escort said. "Joseph doesn't have any other rare skin disease again darling," Alex said. "you aren't interested in being honest with this young woman," Joseph said. Alex was making these other sad faces again folks. Alex was looking into this woman's eye socket again folks. "Joseph is lying to you. Joseph should have felt ashamed of himself. Joseph doesn't have any of that other unknown ailment again sweetheart. Joseph is having intercourse with you. Someone else has accidentally spilled this green hair dye upon my friend's skin again sweetheart. Joseph has done this shit to himself" Alex said. they aren't falling for this guy-friend nonsense anymore. "If you're referring to this alien's race. If you're taking this other stuff out of context again buddy. I'm making these other people kiss my asshole again, buddy," Joseph said. "if you're some dumb-ass bitch. this person isn't very smart again buddy. I'm not like these other dumb asses bitches" this escort said. "You don't know what I'm going to be doing to you? I'm not going to be able to convince them. I'm not becoming this celebrity" Joseph said. "So, if you're permitting me. I'm not having sex with them" Alex said. "If you aren't going to be joining us," the lady said. "Someone else isn't climbing on the top of me. I'm not appointing anyone else. As the leader. I'm not getting involved in this equation again, buddy," Alex said. This escort was looking down at this guy friend's penis again folks. "You wouldn't have minded it again sweetheart. if someone else is thinking about joining us. Because I don't have any problem with it again sweetheart. I love having intercourse with two different gentlemen. I'm finding this stuff exciting to me. If Alex isn't accepting your friend's proposal again buddy. If Alex is the third participant with us. Joseph in this old-fashioned orgy. I'm not sticking my friend. Is Alex at the bottom of the pile? I don't mind sharing my pussy with you" this escort said. "No, I'm not letting my friend's testicles to be dangling in front of my face again darling. Especially if I'm fucking someone else again, darling," Alex said. "No, Because I'm becoming disgusting with them. You won't find this shit obvious to you," Alex said. "If this woman has this other sexually transmitted disease again, buddy. she can try to transmit this other disease to you. Before I'm climbing alongside them" Joseph said. "Before I put my large penis inside of this woman's pussy again, buddy," Alex said. "You can wait another damn minute. I'm fucking this escort" Joseph said. Joseph was shooting his sperm into this poor woman's hair again folks. "Now I'm completing these other tasks of mine. I'm not letting anyone else come up with many of their ideas again sweetheart. they were wiping away this green slime from the edge of this lady's bottom lips again folks. "I'm not allowing anyone else to kiss me. If you aren't noticing, this escort has some of my friend's sperm dripping down both of her lips again, buddy," Alex said. "I'm thinking about my friend's sperm being pasted across this woman's face. You could have done this shit for them. I don't have any more time left again, buddy," Alex said. "You're leaving this place," Joseph said. This woman was climbing out of the bed. This woman has studied

4

# Chapter 4 Closing the Loop

Final Sentencing

*Alex was trying to reserve the two of them a hotel room for tonight. (5 years)*

"If you aren't letting another person, try to do this shit to me. These other people should have gotten this other stuff done in another timely fashion. Because I'm not sure, Alex, if this stuff is over between both of us," Joseph said. These other people aren't making it to their other destinations. Alex was paying another person for these two rooms. This gentleman has remained in his car ever since last night. This person was trying to stop in front of this establishment. So, this person was trying to drop off those two gentlemen near this hotel. "If you aren't interested in reserving for me and you these other hotel rooms. I wasn't able to try to depend on you. I'm not doing these other people any more favors again fella. I'm trying to enter into this different area of this establishment. Because these other people were suspiciously trying to watch both of us. Someone else might have been trying to investigate both of our other endeavors again fella. Do you have any other evil intentions toward another person? I'm not sure if I'm trying to stay here with you overnight. I'm not sure if these other guests are living beside both of us. If another person would have been able to spot both of us. Whenever I'm trying to walk to the outside" Alex said. "I'm not sure if you know this other person's identity again, buddy. If you aren't trying to warn anyone else" Joseph said. Alex was making sure this shit wasn't happening to themselves. Nobody else wasn't interested in trying to follow these two gentlemen outside. "I'm not trying to make these same mistakes with someone else," Alex said. "I'm not sure why another person hasn't been able to comprehend this shit about both of us. If you aren't describing these other things to many of these other people. Alex this other stuff is very disturbing to me. This person was driving this vehicle? If these people weren't able to track our movement in the foreseeable future?" Joseph said. "if you aren't trying to spot this other person's vehicle for us. If this person was trying to head in this direction," Alex said. Joseph wasn't responding to anyone else. "If you're going to become very paranoid about this unknown person's vehicle is trailing behind both of us. Whenever we're traveling down another long stretch of the highway. I was trying to swear under oath that this guy's vehicle is sitting two miles back there again, buddy. I'm not crazy about why these other people behave toward both of us. Maybe If this person has his hood on his vehicle raised in the air" Alex said. I'm not sure if these other people were harboring these other resentful feelings towards these two fugitives. If Joseph was able to persuade another person to take some of those other photographs of themselves. Joseph wasn't concerned with these other people being in their environment. Alex hasn't been aware of many of these other contributing factors again, fellas. If this person is trying to play any sort of significant role in these two fugitives' lives. This person was staring a hole through them. I'm not sure, folks, if this stuff was having a very profound effect on them. This person's vehicle was approaching at a much faster pace. Joseph was trying to convince this other gentleman to press down upon his vehicle's gas pedal. "I'm not trying to pressure you and my partner to try to do anything stupid to anyone else," Alex said. "If you weren't interested in trying to settle down with this woman," the man said. "I'm trying to accompany you into the lobby of this hotel. I'm not trying to pay this employee for renting you and me these two rooms. I'm not sure if this employee is sitting behind this very large desk. I'm trying to bathe myself. I'm trying to take myself this very short nap. If I'm going to try to fall asleep on you," Joseph said. "I'm trying to think about you. I'm not sure how you could have been able to do these other terrible things to another person. I'm trying to come to visit you. If you weren't having any sort of these other delightful dreams about me" Alex said. "You should have been trying to visit me. I'm trying to watch my favorite television host. Before I try to accompany you. Alex into the bedroom. You aren't allowing these other vicious bed bugs to attack me. I'm not sure How you're trying to fuck this person's wife," Joseph said. I'm not trying to have any sort of these other sick fantasies about you," Alex said. "You didn't know about my other intentions toward you. I'm trying to show everyone else that I'm trying to warn them. If you're trying to think about another person trying to kidnap you. If you can't remember the full gist of another person's story. I'm trying to describe most of my other sick dreams to you. You aren't trying to terrorize this young lady's family. If you weren't trying to offer another person this very large amount of your money to proceed with you and your roommate in your other unsavory endeavors again Buddy. So if you're trying to return this young lady's stuff to her other relatives again buddy. I wouldn't have been trying to obey you. You're trying to glue this young lady's panties to my face again, buddy," Joseph said. "I'm getting very sick of your behavior towards them. Because you're trying to make fun at someone else's expense again, buddy. I'm not trying to process the significance of your other dreams again fella. If you're having these dreams of any of those other specific young ladies. You are this very sick person. If you're trying to become this perverted older man. You should have been explaining this stuff to your therapist. Because if you aren't interested in dealing with your other mental illnesses, in my opinion, again, buddy," Joseph said. "I'm not sure why you're trying to play the Victim. Because if you weren't trying to take the bunt of another person joke again, buddy. If you aren't interested in talking to them. Because you're afraid that these other people are going to try to confront you. I'm not sure if they are the same people. Who is insisting that this comedian was out of line with these other devilish jokes about these other people again, Buddy? Kevin Hart doesn't need to make another appearance on another popular television show? They don't want this actor to be the host of any more of those other popular television shows. Kevin Hart has been trying to post these other nasty tweets about these other people's sexuality again, buddy. Kevin was posting these other comments about these other people's sexuality on his Twitter account again, folks. Kevin Hart was banned from performing on another award show in the foreseeable future. Nobody else isn't sure if these other people were calling this award show The Oscars. These other people don't have a very good sense of humor again, folks. These people are very sensitive to these other kinds of inappropriate stuff again Folks? I'm not sure if they are expecting this celebrity to have another opportunity to become this very successful entertainer. If Kevin does have another very poor outlook on his life. If these other actors are making these other unflattering remarks about some of their fellow actors and actresses again, fellas. I'm not sure if these other celebrities would have thought that this world was another awful place to live in again, fellas. If they can't perform their other artistic performance because someone else has become offended by these other celebrities' unflattering remarks about them. If these other people don't know how they can try to prepare themselves for it again, fellas. If they can't try to perform their other jokes in front of another live audience. If they don't know how they should have been to lighten up about this kind of unflattering remarks about themselves. I'm trying to remind you and everyone else that you aren't going to be able to please everyone else in your life. Because I'm not sure if many of those other people are trying to relate to these other stories of mine. I have been writing these other stories of mine for another very long time again, folks. You can't take any of this stuff that I'm saying to these other people to heart again folks. I'm not sure if they found this sort of humor too offensive to them. If I didn't have another chance to offend anyone else. I could have woken you up again, fellas. I'm not sure if these other people would have appreciated my kind of unflattering humor again, fellas.

## *Don Melon was receiving some breaking news folk. (5 years)*

Alex was trying to move towards the direction of the television set. Alex was watching some of his other favorite sitcoms. Alex has these other parents. Who enjoys watching these different types of television programs? Alex was trying to flip through each of these other channels. The executive intends to try to broadcast this content across his other television networks. Alex couldn't have been happier with his favorite anchor. Who was returning to this television show? Don is trying to urge some of these other viewers to tune into this television program. Because Don wants to try to boost the ratings of his show. Don was getting very popular amongst these other young viewers. Who is a part of this sort of demographic again, folks? The executives weren't willing to try to cancel this gentleman's popular show. This executive was trying to broadcast this television show across the world. Alex wasn't interested in trying to fall asleep during the airing of his other favorite shows. Alex was trying to conduct his research into the other likelihoods that there are these other criminal factions. Who was able to try to operate many of their other business dealing with these other terrorist organizations. These sorts of other people are committing these other crimes across this entire city. Alex has been thriving in this particular city. Alex has been able to remain steadfast during these other different periods in his life. Alex was trying to hold onto his same address again folks. Don was trying to report these other newsworthy stories to many of the viewing audience again, folks. "Today, this unknown source has been able to share these interesting developments with me. I have been receiving notifications about this policeman's ongoing investigation against their suspect in this matter again, folks. You might want to cover up both of your children's ears again, folks. I'm trying to warn many of the viewing audience. I have been getting my hands on some of this other very unsettling news again, folks. The sheriff has played every single citizen under another one of his curfews. This sheriff's curfew will go into effect for these surrounding areas of this city. The sheriff is advising everyone else to try to remain indoors. If you are currently trying to travel throughout the city. These two fugitives are still on the run from these other police officers. These other policemen are trying to search for the location of their two fugitives. This sheriff wants to try to remind everyone else. If you're interested in trying to apprehend these two fugitives. These two fugitives are considered to be armed with these other various dangerous weapons again folks. Nobody else should have tried to approach these two fugitives. I'm going to be trying to broadcast this sheriff's press conference on this very television network. If these other reporters do receive another update about the status of these two fugitives and their other heinous crimes against any of these other innocent victims. If I'm going to be able to verify this sort of other information for the viewers of this broadcast. However, someone else has just sent this executive another confirmation that these police officers are going to try to apprehend their two suspects within the next few hours. If you aren't done with trying to shop for these other items again folks. Whenever someone else is making an effort to stop these two fugitives from trying to flee this community. If you're trying to put everyone else lives and their children's lives in serious jeopardy. Because everyone else thinks that they're some sort of modern-day hero. If you're interested in playing the role of these other actors. If you think that you can defeat any of these other villains in some action-filled sort of another movie type of scenario again, folks. These people's chances are getting very slim at this moment again, folks. These other people haven't been able to provide this sheriff with any sort of other information about the whereabouts of their two suspects again folks. You shouldn't have been able to carry any sort of weapon on you. If you don't want to encounter these two fugitives. You should be able to contact your local police department. You shouldn't have been trying to engage in combat with these two suspects. These two fugitives are waiting to try to seriously injure another person. Bruce has been able to dedicate himself and his entire life to this form of martial arts training folks. Bruce is another trained assassin. Bruce possesses an uncanny ability to be able to surpass many of these other individual's fighting skills. Everyone else isn't able to perform these same complex martial arts movements again, folks. if you aren't able to recognize any of these suspects, other victims' faces again, folks. Hillary is this bureaucrat. Hillary is running for the president of the United States of America" Don Melons said. "This person has been accusing these two fugitives of trying to assault him. This medical professional has been able to transport this person to the local hospital. I'm giving everyone else my assessment of this elderly gentleman's current health condition. This elderly gentleman has sustained multiple injuries following his recent altercation with these two fugitives. I'm trying to reach out to this particular individual's legal representation. So I'm going to be asking this lawyer. If he knows the severity of some of his client's other serious injuries again, folks. If this person can give me and these viewers a first-hand account of his altercation with these two fugitives. I'm trying to find out what are these other police officers doing to try to preserve the lives of their citizens. I'm inviting both of those gentlemen to try to make an appearance on my television show" Don Melon said. Don Melon was telling this stuff to these other viewers. Alex was sitting on the couch. "I'm not a member of this terrorist group. I don't know why my favorite television host would like to refer to me as another member of the Mafia. They are calling this organization this insidious Islamic group of thieves. I haven't been targeting these other high-profile individuals. I'm not trying to commit any of their other criminal offenses against anyone else. I'm not partaking in the killing of these two diplomatic leaders with anyone else. I'm not trying to gain influence over anyone else. I don't want to try to control this country's banking system. So they can use the information against them. They were capable of targeting our mayor again folks. I'm not sure if Mayor Johnson is amongst these two fugitive latest casualties again, folks. Sometimes they were capable of targeting these other individuals. They were going to be kidnapping them. They aren't employing anyone else again, folks," Don said. " I'm not accomplishing this mission of mine? They aren't capable of connecting these other dots again, buddy," Alex said. "I'm going to be asking you. If you could wait on me for a minute again, buddy. I'm receiving some breaking news again folks. Someone else was able to bring this shit to my attention again folks. I'm talking to a member of their research committee. This person has been handing me and my co-host another very short memo again folks. I'm not sure if this leader has been sending our affiliates another important message again folks. I should have been allowed to read this memo to you. While I'm still on the air again folks. I'm going to be attempting to read this person's message to you. I'm making an effort to review this person's memo to me. They have been receiving other copies of those crucial documents from them. These government agents haven't been able to apprehend them. Hillary has been able to distribute those other classified documents amongst themselves. Do these people presently reside in the country of Japan?" Don stated, "Hillary was emailing a significant portion of these various documents to them," Don said. Don was looking directly into this cameraman's video camera again folks. Whenever he was saying this stuff to them. "I'm not sure why anyone else is capable of verifying any portion of this guy's story yet again, folks. You shouldn't have been allowed to persuade me. They aren't capable of sending me and anyone else any of this other crucial information to them. I'm trying to verify this information myself. Hillary is pulling the same stunt again folks. I'm trying to reach out to them. I want someone else to be able to ask them. If they aren't capable of providing me and my partner with some of these other specific details about them. I'm contacting this lady and her campaign manager on behalf of our television audience again, folks. I'm not intending for anyone else to be able to approach them. If we aren't playing our customary card game with them. If you aren't expecting me and my friend to bring a bottle of this alcoholic beverage again, darling," stated Don. "I'm not suggesting this stuff to anyone else. I don't know how they were able to play these other adult games with us. Yes, I'm anticipating this nonsense again sweetheart. You aren't bringing any of these other male strippers with you. If Hillary doesn't try to have someone else call off our card game with them. Hillary wasn't capable of making any of those other big decisions for herself" declared Katie. "If Hillary doesn't want anyone else to be canceling her party tonight darling. I'm eager to see them. You didn't know someone else has been fabricating those rumors about me?

*Alex and this weird little creature began discussing the full detail. (5 years)*

Alex was sitting in his abode. Alex was completing many of his other household chores again folks. These two fugitives were going through some of these other hardships throughout their lives. Alex was dealing with this situation himself. Alex doesn't participate in those types of activities with many of his other friends. Alex isn't helping to make this creature's plans come to fruition anytime soon again, fellas. Alex isn't going to be speaking to this creature about his other issues with certain people. Alex has been discussing these other topics with this creature. Alex was putting this creature's telephone calls on hold again, folks. Alex wasn't going to be able to try to overcome his other shortcomings in his life again, folks. Alex prevented this creature from trying to achieve many of his objectives again, folks. Alex was going to be facing many of those other obstacles by himself. Joseph has been impeding upon this young man. Alex wasn't trying to establish these other typical relationships with these groups of other gentlemen's wives. Alex wasn't comparing this creature's and his other bad habits to another person and their bad habits again fellas. Alex didn't receive these other women's proposals to try to go out on any romantic dinner date with them. These women were constantly rejecting this young man's romantic advance towards them. Alex has been developing this other lack of motivation within himself. Alex isn't interested in trying to take advantage of these other systemic processes again, folks. Alex is trying to require these other deep understanding of this creature. Because Alex wasn't trying to operate this entire system on another daily basis again fellas. Joseph has been subjecting this young man to these other stringent routines. I'm not sure if Joseph was making this stuff harder on this young man. These other people were trying to offer these fugitives these other rare opportunities again, folks. Alex wasn't preparing to be able to deal with this stuff for anyone else. Alex isn't trying to embark on another mission alongside anyone else again, folks. Alex wasn't receiving any sort of pleasure from trying to perform this kind of unacceptable work for someone else again, fellas. Alex wasn't trying to implement these other people's ideas into another work-related environment again, fellas. Alex isn't interested in trying to explore these other different avenues for this creature. Alex wasn't trying to satisfy these other unnatural cravings for this creature. Alex was trying to pursue these moments of these other fleeing pleasures again, folks. Alex wasn't sure if this stuff was an ongoing occurrence during his lifetime. Alex has been struggling with this significant amount of this creature, causing havoc in these other people's lives again, folks. Alex isn't interested in trying to illustrate his other concepts to this creature. Joseph wasn't interested in trying to grasp the meaning behind many of this young man's current concepts again fellas. Joseph wasn't interested in providing this young man with his perspectives on this topic again fellas. I'm trying to use some of this other creativity of mine. I'm trying to create a little more captivating plot for many of these other readers. I'm trying to create some of these other characters. I'm creating these other characters to be a little more diverse in their thinking about certain political issues and these other politicians, again, fellas. Alex has been my main character in this story of mine. I have created this character to become a more authentic version of myself. So I'm trying to bring these sorts of characters to the forefront of my story. If these other characters can't grab the attention of these other readers again, folks. Then, I haven't been able to perfectly execute my main objectives of building a more convincing set of these other characters again, fellas. I'm sure as the narrator of this story. I think that folks, it is my fault that these other people don't understand the significance of my story or its theme again, fellas. So if these other people aren't interested in remaining silent throughout this entire process of mine. I have failed you. So I'm going to try to continue telling everyone else this story of mine. Alex wasn't able to try to engage in any sort of other sexual activities with many of these other females. If Alex can't find another potential mate for himself. Alex wasn't sure if he believed in the existence of another civilization. Alex has been unsure of this sort of topic again fellas. I'm not sure if there are these other species living in the universe. Alex has been able to try to study these other species' mating habits with their counterparts. Do you believe in the existence of another species? These other people weren't living on this other massive asteroid again fellas? Joseph isn't trying to use these different resources to sustain his life. If Joseph can't find the material to manufacture this fertilizer again fellas. So Joseph can try to grow these other crops during these other warmer seasons? These other species weren't trying to survive on this planet. Alex doesn't realize that this creature doesn't care about anyone's else life again, fellas. Joseph is the only person. who is trying to do this other crap to this young man? They were being presented with these different resolutions themselves. Alex was going to end this conflict between these people. Joseph wasn't interested in being another predecessor to everyone else. Alex wasn't trying to condone anyone else foolishness again fellas. I'm not sure, Joseph was this very dominating force in this young person's life. Alex wasn't trying to tolerate this stuff from anyone else. this person was trying to put this creature on notice for some of his other ridiculous ranting about how they are raising their other children. Alex is turning this situation between him and his roommate into another very hostile pissing contest again fellas. Alex hasn't authorized another person to try to help himself. Alex isn't interested in trying to adjust to these other sequences of events anymore, folks. Alex wouldn't have allowed another person to maim his pet again fellas. If Alex isn't interested in trying to use these other methods on this creature. Alex could have been able to produce a much better outcome between himself and his roommate. Alex hasn't tried to persuade this creature to try to settle this dispute between both of them. Alex could have used a different approach to try to gain the trust of this creature again fellas. Joseph doesn't believe in these other several elements of someone else's life. Joseph doesn't feel like trying to answer another person's questions about him and his roommate searching for the location of the Holy Grail. Joseph isn't interested in discovering another diverse civilization. Joseph wasn't interested in taking this young man's perspective on this sort of topic very lightly again, folks. Especially if Joseph is trying to do these other unpleasant things to these other people. Joseph wasn't interested in participating in these similar activities with this young man. Alex has been able to attract these different things to himself. Joseph doesn't share these same attributes with this young man. Alex is trying to correspond with this creature. Joseph shouldn't have been ridiculing another person for not trying to share his perspective on certain topics again fellas. Is Alex trying to travel alongside this creature on this journey? Alex wasn't sure if this creature was trying to create another successful business endeavor with someone else. Alex is trying to speculate about this sort of topic again fellas. Alex isn't interested in trying to solve this creature's problem for him. Alex hasn't been trying to do anything improper to anyone else. Joseph was getting very furious with this creature. Joseph wasn't interested in trying to influence anyone else opinion of his other mission on this planet. Alex wasn't interested in participating in these other unsavory activities with this creature. Alex was presenting these other preparations to these other people. Alex was very observant of the creature's behavior towards certain people. Joseph wasn't interested in trying to incorporate these different techniques into his life. Joseph wasn't interested in trying to advance another person's agenda for them. Joseph wasn't interested in trying to cooperate with these other people. These other people weren't sure if this creature policy would have affected their children's sovereign state of mind. Alex wasn't interested in trying to have another conversation with someone else. how this creature has been able to create these other unfortunate mishaps in his life again, fellas? Joseph is interested in trying to create these different types of inventions for the betterment of the entire population. Those other types of people weren't a part of this different environment. Joseph has been trying to convince this other person to complete this task for him. Joseph was interested in trying to perpetrate these other heinous acts against his other victims. If Alex is interested in trying to inquire about this creature's other intentions toward these other individuals. Joseph doesn't have this young man wrapped around his very tiny little finger anymore, fellas. Alex has been holding onto another grudge against this creature for quite a while now. Alex was interested in trying to make these other decisions for this creature. Alex is interested in trying to sabotage this creature this weekend. Joseph was interested in trying to destroy this young man's life. Joseph wasn't interested in trying to make another very huge announcement in front of this young man. "I'm not interested in trying to let another person use my ability against these other victims. I'm not this puppet. Who is working alongside someone else in this very large carnival" Alex said.

9 781639 503162